New York Engagement

CARPE DIEM CHRONICLES 1.5

MAIDA MALBY

EOT Publications

COPYRIGHT

ACKNOWLEDGMENTS

To my husband B and our son Stevie, for always inspiring and supporting me.

To my editor Linda Hill, for giving me proper guidance. This could have gone so differently if you had not shown me the way.

To Trish Smith, for brainstorming the plot with me.

To my high school *kabarkada* Dr. Love Mariano and Grace Soriano, for the expert medical consult.

To my Beta Readers Milly Bellegris, Gena Gilliam, Sue Schober, and Violet Olivo, for your invaluable input. You improved my story tremendously.

To my cover artist Lucy Rhodes, for finding Krista in New York. I adore working with you. You're so spot on and we're super in-sync. I always look forward to our working chats.

To Tessa Dare, for giving me the idea for Krista's back story.

Thank you all. *Maraming salamat.*

DEDICATION

To my OSRBC friends, here's to Reading More Diverse Romance.

MAIDA MALBY

CHAPTER ONE

Empire State

Deborah Kerr is right, Krista thought. *The Empire State Building* is *the nearest thing to heaven in New York City.* The bright lights of The City That Never Sleeps twinkled before her from the 86th-floor open-air observation deck of what was once the tallest building in the world. Snow blanketed the floor beneath her and the rooftops nearby, creating a winter wonderland of enchantment. Despite the bracing air, inside she felt warm, joyful.

Krista stepped away from the railing to rest her head on the hard chest of the man who was the primary reason for her contentment. Blake stood behind her, patiently allowing her to take in her fill of his birthplace. Her pulse skittered when he wrapped his arms around her and clasped both of her gloved hands in his.

"Cold?" he asked, his hold on her tightening when she shivered.

Krista shook her head. "No, I'm fine. I'm warm and toasty." Between the protection of her coat and the heat from his big body, she spoke the truth. His nearness made her tingle, not the wind of the frosty night, four days before Christmas.

They'd been together for nearly two months, but she still marveled at her body's reaction to him. At their office in Makati, she never had to turn around or look to check whether he was in the same room. She had developed a sixth sense when it came to Blake Ryan.

Before they found themselves falling in love in Boracay, she had avoided being close to him, had made it a point to keep her distance. He was her boss, a foreigner, an American: someone Krista knew her mother wouldn't approve of. Marissa Lopez's own experience with an American, who she'd only known by the name "John," had left her alone, pregnant, and full of shame. She didn't want the same for her eldest daughter. But Krista's heart wanted Blake. His wanted her.

They had arrived only a few hours ago, exhausted by the long trip from the Philippines. Still, knowing jet lag would hit them hard later, they had opted to acclimatize to the time zone and weather. Krista and Blake decided to stay awake after checking in at their hotel and taking a quick shower. They'd descended to the lobby of The Plaza Hotel in search of food. Luckily, the Food Hall one level below still had some open shops.

Blake nudged her hood aside to whisper in her ear. "I can hear the wheels turning around in your head. What are you thinking of?"

"Food." She turned and grinned when she caught her boyfriend's surprised look.

"You want to eat again?" His eyes roamed all over her face, as if looking for signs of hunger.

She gave his chest a light tap. The supple leather covering her hand made the action totally harmless. "No, silly. I can still taste that absolutely yummy dinner from Luke's. I wasn't hungry before we ate, but I swear, I could have devoured two of those lobster rolls. They were so buttery, so mouth-wateringly sweet, juicy and oh ... so ... luscious." She closed her eyes, licked her lips, and moaned at the remembered satisfaction. When she opened her eyes, Blake was staring at her mouth, his own eyes blazing with blue fire.

He abruptly let go of her and started buttoning his coat. His fingers, clumsy in their haste, misaligned the top button. Then he reached for her hand and pulled her behind him, his strides long and hurried.

"Where are we going?" She tugged to slow him down.

"Hotel." Brusque and short.

Oh! She noted the flush in his cheeks and the glow in his eyes. Her lips tilted up in a knowing smile. She darted past him.

When they stepped into the elevator, Blake went to the corner and positioned her in front of him, her back plastered to his front. Through the thickness of her coat, the rigid column of his erection nestled against her bottom.

"Bed," he growled in her ear.

Krista trembled as answering desire flowed through her. The sensuality he'd always evoked in her won over the fatigue of travel.

The trip back to the hotel was a blur. No words passed their lips; they were fused in a frenzied kiss that lasted the duration of the ride. Only the abrupt breaking of the taxi and the curt announcement, "The Plaza," forced them apart. Blake handed a twenty to the smirking driver and hustled Krista out without waiting for change.

As intent on getting to their room as she was, she still shook her head over Blake's excessive generosity. She didn't begrudge the driver the huge tip. It hadn't been that long since her family was considered poor—only two years. She understood the need for every bit of bonus she could earn by working overtime. If they got married, she'd have to get used to Blake's casual extravagance.

Not if, but when. In Boracay, Krista had doubted Blake's love for her. She'd thought his declaration had come too fast, too soon. But he had shown her during the past eight weeks, in both words and deeds, that his feelings for her were true and steadfast.

As the chief executive officer of the company they both worked for, he hadn't allowed any censure of their relationship. With her agreement, he had pronounced them a couple at the general assembly and followed the announcement with a warning that gossip and malicious rumors would be dealt with in an appropriate manner.

The ping of the elevator door opening to their floor brought her to the present.

"About damned time," Blake grumbled as they stepped out and dashed to their room. He smiled at her sheepishly when she laughed out loud.

Krista reached up to plant a kiss on his chin as he fumbled with the key card. Tall for a Filipina and wearing high-heeled boots, she didn't have to stretch far. "Patience is a virtue you do *not* have, Mr. Blake Ryan."

She stepped back to remove her coat while he opened the door. Blake's own jacket and scarf were already hanging over his arm. She let out a yelp when he grabbed her by the waist and backed her into their room.

"You're calling me impatient?" He dropped his armload of clothes on the floor and lifted her. Four quick steps took them to the middle of the room. "I'll show you impatience," he declared, throwing her onto the massive king-sized bed and diving over her. His ardent kiss silenced Krista's squeal.

His mouth ravaged hers, his tongue relentless. She matched his urgency stroke for stroke. Her hands were busy with his belt as his occupied themselves with her bra. When he lifted his head to catch his breath, she shifted to the side to remove her top and unfasten her belt. Blake hastily undressed, kicking off his shoes and socks, unzipping his pants, and stepping out of them in a handful of rapid moves. Seeing her struggle with her over-the-knee boots, he took over their removal while she wiggled out of her jeans and panties.

"Aah, love, you are so beautiful." Blake's gaze worshiped her as she held out her arms to urge him back to her. She wanted him close, craved his weight on top of her. Her nipples were pebbled to hard points and between her legs, arousal dampened her nether lips. She parted her thighs in blatant invitation.

"So are you, honey." Her breath caught when he mounted the bed and held his cock in one hand. His thumb spread the moisture on the fleshy tip. The bed had been turned down and the lamps lit; their soft glow illuminated her lover's magnificent body. Krista lifted her hands in clear appeal. "Blake, please make love with me."

He spread her legs wider to make space for himself. When he knelt in front of her, she wrapped her legs around him and crossed her ankles at the small of his back. Clutching his shoulders, Krista lifted her upper body, needing to feel him skin to skin.

"Easy, baby." Blake calmed her even as he raised her hips to receive him. He drove into her, his thrust made easy by her liquid heat. They had long-past eschewed the use of condoms. Both wanted the increased closeness of going flesh to flesh. They were both healthy, and she'd been on the pill even before they became intimately involved.

"So good. Blake, more. Hurry." She rocked against him, each instinctive move bringing carnal delight to them both. Her breathing rasped; it hitched as his thrust reached deep. His retreat brought forth a plaintive moan from her; it quickly turned into a purr with his return.

"Come for me, sweetheart." Blake crooned the order near her ear before he nibbled at her lower lip. In sharp contrast to his gentle tone, his shaft slid in and out of her drenched channel with frantic speed.

Krista couldn't help but comply. Her climb to the peak of pleasure was aided, urged by his magical hands. With her nails digging into his muscled back she reached the crest, gasping for breath at its intensity. He soon followed, his essence flowing into her in a hot, pulsating stream.

CHAPTER TWO

The Plaza

Blake sat up in bed, uncertain what woke him. He glanced at the window to gauge the time. No help there. Beyond the drawn white curtains, he only saw gray; the glass facade of the opposite building reflected hardly any light. As much as he wished their room overlooked Central Park, their late booking had defeated that choice.

His gaze moved to Krista, and his face bloomed in a wide smile. *She'd* woken him, the bed hog. Krista lay on her right side diagonally across the king-sized bed, facing him. Her long hair formed a black cloud on the white pillow, and the blanket covered her to her neck. Only her left fist, clutching the cotton bedcover, was visible. She must have kicked out when she turned.

Blake reached out to touch her hand. She didn't wear much jewelry. Either a pair of small gold stud earrings or the crimson pearls he'd given her in Boracay. He'd lucked out when the ring in the matched set of pearls had fit her finger. He knew what size to get for her at Tiffany's.

He had no idea when he'd have the chance to slip into the famous Fifth Avenue store to buy her engagement ring, or when and where he'd propose. Their schedule had them doing everything together twenty-four seven for the next two weeks.

This kind of uncertainty unnerved him. In the Philippines he had a reputation for being decisive and in control. Apparently, those qualities didn't hold true in New York. He decided more sleep might help.

As Blake lay back down, his cell phone vibrated on the bedside table. He reached for it before it woke Krista.

Blake's heart slammed against his ribcage when he saw his older brother's name on the screen, along with five missed calls. He swung his feet onto the floor as he said into the receiver, "Is it Ma?"

"Uncle Jack was stabbed outside the pub. Medics rushed him to the ER," Aidan barked with no preamble.

Shit! Though relieved that it wasn't either of his parents, he worried equally for his Da's best friend and business partner.

"Where is everybody?" Blake turned the phone to face the room, to light his way to the bathroom.

"I'm riding along with Ronan. The suspect's still at large. Ma and Da are at the hospital now with *Tita* Belen. Craig is still in the air. ETA three hours. Darcy won't arrive until twelve hundred hours. Patrick has gone AWOL."

Blake made a note of which hospital to go to and promised to be there in fifteen minutes. If neither Ronan nor Patrick could be there to support Uncle Jack and *Tita* Belen, Blake would take their place in the meantime.

He got dressed, grabbing whatever he could reach and deciding by feel rather than style. Once done, he returned to the bed.

Krista remained undisturbed by all the noise and the light he'd turned on in the closet. Despite the gravity of the situation, Blake smiled at his girlfriend. She had always slept like the dead. Fatigue from the flight and their lovemaking had depleted her energy; she needed this time to recharge. With regret, he leaned down to wake her.

"Krista, sweetheart." He cupped a hand over her shoulder, giving it a gentle shake. Groaning, she rolled all the way over to the other side. "Baby, I have to go." He pulled the blanket off, knowing the loss of warmth would get her attention. She flopped onto her back and squinted at him.

"What time is it?" she croaked. Tugging the blanket up to cover her nudity, she sat up and reached for the bottled water on the bedside table. "Why are you dressed?"

He waited until she'd taken a sip before replying. "It's past three a.m. I have to go to the hospital." At her gasp, he explained quickly. "Uncle Jack is in the ER. I don't know what his condition is, but Aidan was worried enough to call."

She scrambled off the bed and grabbed the hotel robe from the floor. "I'm going with you. Give me five minutes." Without waiting for his response, Krista headed for the bathroom.

He followed as soon as he heard the toilet flush. "Are you sure, sweetheart?" He raised his voice to be heard over the sound of her brushing her teeth. "We could be sitting there waiting for hours. You can stay here and catch up on sleep." No response, just the sound of running water and splashing.

She came out with her face gleaming, moisture still clinging to the baby-fine strands of hair on her forehead. Smudges darkened the skin beneath her eyes, but she looked alert and wide awake.

"I wouldn't be able to go back to sleep anyway. I'll only worry while you're gone. If I go with you, you won't have to check in with me every few hours." She walked briskly to the closet.

True to her word, she came out in five minutes wearing a pair of jeans and a red cashmere sweater.

Even though the employees christened their office "The Siberia of Bonifacio Global City" for the air-conditioner setting of seventeen degrees Celsius, it still hadn't prepared Krista for the arctic frigidity of The Big Apple during wintertime.

Since none of the department stores in the Philippines carried winter clothes, they'd used every minute of their two-hour layover in Hong Kong to outfit Krista with basic attire for the winter weather in New York. Her coat and the sweater she wore now were among those purchases.

They'd had a brief battle over who'd pay for the mini shopping spree. His stubbornly independent girlfriend had insisted on paying for all the clothes and only allowed him to give her the footwear. Blake declared himself the winner in the skirmish because the black stretch suede Jimmy Choo boots with embellished heels that now encased her long legs had cost him nearly two thousand dollars.

Reaching into his pocket, he rubbed a one-peso coin between his fingers. She'd handed it to him to counter the superstition regarding his gift of footwear. His lips lifted in amusement at the incongruity of that action.

"What are you smiling about?" Krista poked his chin in inquiry. She had donned her gloves and coat, slung a purse over her shoulder, and looked ready to go on his signal.

Pulling her close, he placed a soft kiss on her forehead. "You. Have I told you how amazing you are?" Her eyes flashed with pleasure at his compliment.

"Every day. And so are you. I don't tell you often enough." Leaning in for a kiss, she breathed against his mouth, "You're magnificent, Blake. I love you."

Incredibly happy with her words, he met her sweet lips with his own. He'd been the first one to say, "I love you," but she was fast making up for lost time.

***

Krista watched the multitude of glittering lights on the facades of the towering buildings as the taxi traveled westward along 59th Street. The holiday season's demand for gaudier displays likely multiplied the expected luminescence a hundredfold. Even the numerous groves of trees in Central Park were festooned with star-like pinpoints of illumination.

At this time of the morning traffic flowed easily, and the streets were devoid of pedestrians. A quick check on the weather app on her phone told her it was sixteen degrees Fahrenheit. Minus-nine degrees Celsius. *Brrrr.* No wonder even the homeless kept out of the harsh elements. *The city sleeps after all.*

Blake broke into her thoughts. "Are you nervous?"

"About meeting your family in person?" A smile broke over her face when she remembered how nervous Blake had been upon meeting her parents and siblings. Correction: anxious. Blake confessed to having been anxious. "A little bit." She had "met" the older Ryans online when Blake told them via a video call that he was bringing her to New York. The only ones she hadn't met yet were Craig and Darcy. The Ryans would all be present in New York City for their annual family reunion.

"Don't be. You've met Aidan. He's the worst of the lot," he joked.

"I like Aidan." The oldest Ryan son had the same birthday as Krista: November 2. They'd celebrated it together in Boracay when he came to visit from Singapore. "I'm scared of him, but I like him."

"There you go! No worries then." Blake idly played with the ends of her ponytailed hair. "My parents already love you because I do. Craig is a goofy teddy bear. And Darcy is a nerd, like you." He snickered.

She playfully punched him in the arm. It was the truth. She couldn't dispute that.

"Tell me more about your Uncle Jack."

What she knew so far about the couple was that Blake's Uncle Jack and *Tita* Belen had been together for nearly thirty years. The Irish-American and Filipina couple intrigued her. In her mind, they were the model of how a marriage could work between such a mixed pairing: those couples she knew in the Philippines were all divorced. She hoped most fervently that she and Blake would have as strong a relationship in the future. He was her first love. And in her heart, the last.

"Uncle Jack was my brother's idol. He's why Aidan joined the US Air Force instead of any other branch of the military. Uncle Jack got injured in Saudi Arabia during Operation Desert Storm and was honorably discharged. He brought *Tita* Belen and their two sons when he came home to New York from the Philippines.

"My dad was looking for a partner for the bar, and it seemed the perfect solution for everyone, especially because *Tita* Belen was a cook by profession."

Krista stilled. "Your Uncle Jack was assigned to the Philippines in the late eighties? He was at Clark Air Force Base? John, my biological father, was assigned there too. Maybe they knew each other."

"I'm not entirely sure where Uncle Jack was stationed. I believe *Tita* Belen is from Palawan. I never had cause to ask more about their story. Uncle Jack could have been vacationing there and that's how he and *Tita* Belen met."

The taxi passed a twenty-four-hour coffee shop and glided to a stop just past the corner.

"We're here." Blake's announcement startled her.

Already? It took only five minutes to get there. If it had been later in the day, they could have walked, but not during the wee hours of the morning.

No sooner had they entered the hospital than a couple rushed towards them. Blake's parents, Krista realized. Removing her hand from Blake's grasp, she held back, wanting to give the family their reunion time.

"Blake! I'm so happy you're home." Giulia Ryan's arms opened wide to welcome her son. "I missed you so much," she wept against his chest when he leaned down to wrap her in a tight embrace.

"Ma, don't cry," Blake admonished as he wiped the tears away from his mother's face ever so tenderly. "You see me practically every week when we video chat."

Mrs. Ryan sniffed. "That's different. I can't hug you there like this."

"Giulia, my heart, let your son go and greet this lovely young lady he brought home to us." Sean Ryan's deep basso suited his heavy frame perfectly. Blake's dad approached Krista as he spoke. Before she could hold out her hand, Sean had her enveloped in a hug, his warmth completely obliterating any anxieties she felt about meeting her boyfriend's parents.

She felt a tug on one beefy arm before being squeezed by the shorter, softer Ryan. Krista returned the embrace, marveling at the strength of a woman who barely reached the height of her shoulders. At only five feet tall, plump, and smelling of chocolate, Giulia Ryan was the very definition of cuddly.

Krista was hesitant to let go of the older woman but her awkward stance of bent knees and hunched shoulders got so uncomfortable, she might have toppled at any moment. Thankfully, Blake came to her side and held her as she gently extricated herself from his mom's embrace.

"Oh, Krista, how pretty you are. The video camera didn't do you justice." Mrs. Ryan beamed at her.

Krista blushed at the effusive praise. She wasn't used to being complimented for her looks. Before Blake, she had played them down, had covered her curves. She had wanted to be recognized for her intelligence, not for her beauty. He'd seen through her mask and still pursued her.

"How was your flight? Blake didn't tell us anything when he called. He only said you've arrived."

"Ma, before you grill Krista, can we first find somewhere to sit? We're still a little jet-lagged. Also, how's Uncle Jack, and where is *Tita* Belen?" His arm casually slung over her shoulder, Blake drew Krista away from his mother.

Sean answered. "Before we came out to meet you, Jack was still in surgery. Belen is waiting for word from his doctor. We'll take you to the ER waiting room; that's where we told her we'd meet her once she's had news."

CHAPTER THREE

Central Park

Blake steered Krista around the harried medical staff and the loudly complaining injured in the waiting area of the emergency room. After escorting her to a chair, he sat on the adjoining hard plastic seat and pulled her close.

Krista gazed over his shoulder to his parents, who he knew were ambling away to get some coffee. "Your Ma and Da are wonderful. What should I call them?"

Blake was stumped for an answer. He knew Filipinos could not bring themselves to address people who were older than them by their given name. They always had to use an honorific to show respect. He was invited to call Krista's parents *Tito* Arsen and *Tita* Marissa, and though he had used the Filipino words for uncle and aunt occasionally, he was more comfortable addressing them as Sir and Ma'am.

Scratching his head, he met his girlfriend's enquiring gaze, then the answer came to him. *Of course.* "You can call them Ma and Da, like I do."

Krista's eyes shone. "Oh, Blake. Truly?"

"Yes. I want you to treat them like they're your parents, too."

"Blake, you're home!" Beneath his hand, Krista's spine straightened at the overfamiliarity in the female voice. He rubbed her back in reassurance before rising to greet the most important Filipina in his life prior to meeting Krista.

"*Tita* Belen." He stepped forward to give his honorary aunt a hug. "How are you holding up?" he asked when they parted.

His aunt seemed thinner than the last time he saw her, a year ago. For a cook, she was unusually skinny. Today she appeared gaunt, brittle. And older, too. Lines stretched over her forehead; they bracketed both sides of her eyes and mouth. He held both of her hands in his. Her eyes were watery. Panic seized him. "Is Uncle Jack—"

"Oh, Blake! John is in a coma." Tears fell, seemingly unnoticed, down her face. "The doctor said he ... lost a lot of blood, not just from the ... stabbing, but also from the head injury he got when he ... fell." The last word came out in a hiccup. He caught her in his arms as she collapsed.

He sent a helpless glance to Krista. She stood and inclined her head towards the chair, suggesting he set his aunt down.

"*Tita* Belen, why don't we—" He'd kept his tone low and gentle. Maybe a bit too gentle. She clung to him tighter, as if by getting closer she could absorb some of his strength. He awkwardly patted her back.

"Mrs. O'Connor." Krista spoke softly, one hand resting lightly on Belen's shoulder. She held a pack of tissues in the other hand.

His aunt's head came up sharply from its place on his chest, and a mask of astonishment wreathed her features when she caught sight of the speaker. Krista spoke perfect English, if slightly accented. The way she pronounced the short "i" as the long "e" sound and kept the "o"s instead of making it sound like "er" betrayed her Filipino roots.

"Maire?" *Tita* Belen staggered backward and plopped down with a thud, her eyes never leaving Krista's face. She shook her head as if to deny the vision in front of her. Brows knotted, eyes narrowed, she asked, "You're not— Who are you?"

Bothered by the sharp tone in his aunt's voice, Blake draped his arm across Krista's waist. "*Tita* Belen, I would like you to meet Krista, my girlfriend."

"Girlfriend? How come you never told me about her?"

Huh? They were close, but he and his aunt didn't have the kind of relationship that would have him seek her out to update her about his life. He left those kinds of catching-up activities for when they met in person, usually during their annual reunion at Christmas. "I figured Ma would tell you."

"Oh, my dear Belen!" Speaking of the devil, his parents had returned from their coffee run. "What did the doctor say?"

His father waved him to a seat adjacent to where *Tita* Belen and Ma sat. He led Krista there and accepted the coffee from his dad. The tail-end of his aunt's update to his mother about Uncle Jack's condition caught his attention.

"... blood donors."

"Does Uncle Jack need a transfusion? I can donate. I'm O negative, the universal donor."

"Thank you, Blake. I'm sure the hospital can use that, but the doctor said he needs B negative. The boys and I are all O negative. John is the only one with a different blood type."

Krista gasped. Her hand, which rested on Blake's leg, gripped his jeans, and her nails dug into the denim cloth. With voice just above a whisper, as if talking more to herself, she said, "I'm B negative." Uttered low, only he heard it.

Krista and Uncle Jack had the same blood type? *What an odd coincidence.* But could she even donate?

Leaning close to her so that nobody else could hear, he said, "But, baby, you just got a tattoo."

"So?"

"They might not accept your blood because you got your ink overseas. That tattoo parlor is not licensed according to US standards."

"I want to try. You saw how sterile the artist kept her equipment, how clean the studio was. She used new needles and fresh ink. I'm certain my blood will pass the test."

Facing her, he caressed her cheek. "Are you sure you want to do this?"

She glanced at *Tita* Belen for a few seconds before nodding. "Yes, I want to help. Please don't tell your aunt."

It disappointed Blake that *Tita* Belen hadn't taken to Krista as well as he'd thought she would. He'd expected their shared Filipino heritage would make them bond. Instead, his aunt was cold, bordering on hostile. He didn't know what caused it, but now wasn't the time to find out. Perhaps Krista was right to keep her donation a secret until they knew that the gift would be appreciated.

He brushed a kiss on Krista's forehead and said, "Okay, sweetheart. I'll see what I can do. Will you wait here? I'll check what the process is." At her nod, he moved to tell his father where he was going and to ask him to watch over Krista. He didn't want to leave her by herself, but they couldn't afford to waste time.

If Uncle Jack urgently needed Krista's blood as his wife had said, Blake would make sure he'd receive it.

CHAPTER FOUR

Midtown

"Bl—" Krista whispered, her hand reaching out to his departing form. *Come back.* He didn't hear her. She hadn't expected him to.

Bereft of Blake's comforting presence, Krista wrapped her arms about herself. It wasn't cold in the waiting room; the heater blasted, but she shivered, nonetheless. The coffee wouldn't have helped, either. She wasn't allowed to drink it, not if she was going to give blood later. When she'd donated before, Krista was told that caffeine was a diuretic and could cause dehydration.

She snuck a peek at Blake's parents, their heads close together, talking to their friend. They looked like a unit, a family.

It's good I'm donating blood, otherwise I might as well have just stayed at the hotel. A wave of homesickness crashed into her. She took out her phone to check the current time in the Philippines. Five in the afternoon. Her parents would still be at their café, busy serving travelers who were on their way to the province of Quezon for the Christmas holidays.

"Nope, not the best timing," she muttered to herself.

What would she tell them anyway? That she had the same blood type as an American? A US Air Force veteran who had spent time in the Philippines during the late eighties, but not necessarily at Clark? There were probably hundreds, even thousands, who could answer to the same description.

What did he even look like? He could be a redhead, or he could be black. Easy enough to check. Krista pressed her index finger to the home button on her phone. It lit up with a text message telling her she had connected to a US network.

Of its own volition it seemed, her finger tapped the search engine. Over the tab "Images," she typed "Jack O'Connor, Ryan O'Connor Pub and Restaurant." She shut her eyes before the photos flashed on-screen.

"Taking a nap?"

Krista wasn't sure which moved faster, her hand to throw the phone into her purse, or her eyes as they snapped open to behold the oldest Ryan. She had been so engrossed in her task, she hadn't noticed him move to sit beside her.

"Uhm, just resting my eyes," she said. Truth be told, she'd welcome the chance to close her eyes for ten more hours.

"I wouldn't blame you if you were." Sean shifted in his seat, his bulk nearly occupying two of the plastic chairs. "Even though it's been four years since we traveled to the Philippines, I still remember the jetlag that hit me afterwards. Giulia told me my snores rivaled the sirens on the streets. How she heard that, I'll never know. She was as deeply asleep as I was."

His grin was so contagious, Krista couldn't help but return it with a wide smile of her own. "Where did Blake take you when you went? How long did you stay? Was that your first time there?"

The feeling of desolation left her, replaced by a burst of love for Blake's parents. So deep was her gratitude, she had to hide her hands in her coat pockets to stop herself from throwing her arms around Blake's father and declaring her everlasting love.

Sean threw back his head and boomed out a guffaw. Krista wanted to shush him, but a quick look around the room told her no one was paying attention or taking offense.

"Young lady, you're delightful. We went to Makati and toured the walled city in Manila—Intramuros, I think is what you call it?" At her nod, he continued. "Then, we went to Boracay. Blake didn't have his resort yet, but we saw the potential. White Beach was fine for the young ones, but for old coots like me, nope." He thumped his chest with a meaty fist, so heavily that it would have felled a smaller person; it barely moved him at all.

"Who are you calling old? Not me, I hope." From her perch beside Belen, Giulia teased her husband.

"Not you, *mo chroi*. You're forever young." Sean blew his wife a kiss, making her giggle, shedding years off her face.

My heart. Krista smiled at the Irish endearment. One of her favorite romance authors came from Ireland and often used such terms in her books.

"We also went to Zambales and Pampanga. To Mount Pinatubo and the former US bases there: Subic and Clark. Jack talked often about his assignment there; we had to see for ourselves."

Krista's eyes rounded. Her heart thumped in her throat. "Mr. O'Connor was based in Clark? When?" she croaked out.

"Mid-to-late eighties, until it closed in ninety-one. He was assigned briefly to Saudi Arabia during the first Gulf War, but Belen and the boys stayed in the Philippines. Why do you ask?" Sean inquired gently.

"Uhm. I was born in Pampanga. My parents used to live in Angeles City, a few miles outside the base." She could barely get the words out. Her mouth was dry.

"Ah. It never ceases to amaze me how small the world is. We're fortunate to have the opportunities we've had to travel and explore places we've never been before. With the boys choosing to live in Southeast Asia, I think we'll have more chances to see your beautiful region."

Krista nodded, relieved that Sean hadn't pursued the opening she provided to probe more into her family history. Her mind and heart warred over what to do with all the coincidences that kept popping up.

She snuck a glance towards Belen O'Connor. She'd called her husband "John." Wasn't that the convention here in the US? Like President Kennedy. Wasn't his real name John, but everybody called him Jack? As if sensing Krista's scrutiny, the older woman threw a resentful glare at her before turning her face away.

She hates me. How disappointing. She had held the older woman in high regard, even before they'd met. This wasn't how it was supposed to be between them. She and Belen should have been great friends. Instead, they weren't even talking. Blake's honorary aunt couldn't even bring herself to look Krista in the eye.

If Krista wanted to confirm her ever-increasing suspicions regarding Jack O'Connor, no support would be forthcoming from *that* corner. She had to do it alone. Not totally, of course. Blake would help. In fact, he had already started.

Even if Jack turned out to be a total stranger, Krista felt justified in giving her blood to him. She would have done it for any one of her friends' loved ones. She would do it for Blake and those he considered family.

"Krista, sweetie, it's kind of you to come and offer support. Isn't that right, Belen?" Giulia's not-so-subtle inquiry held mild rebuke.

The response was begrudgingly polite. "Yes, thank you, Krista."

"Please don't mention it, Mrs. O'Connor. You and your husband are important to Blake, and now to me as well."

Giulia waved a hand in the air. "What's all this formality then? You must call them *Tita* Belen and Uncle Jack, like all my kids do."

No wonder Blake feared his mother. Krista had never met a more decisive woman. Obviously, her boyfriend had inherited his managing ways from her. Aidan, too. They must have learned from the cradle.

"That's fine with me," Belen agreed, then stood abruptly. "Excuse me. I'll check on John." Without waiting for a response, she left the three of them gaping at her.

Giulia turned to Krista, her brows knotted in puzzlement. "She's distraught. Belen is usually ..." She trailed off, giving a helpless shrug.

Krista understood. Anything Giulia added would only magnify Belen's rude behavior towards her. For a second, Krista considered being petty by remaining silent and letting Giulia think poorly of her friend. But that would shame her mother and all that she'd taught her daughter.

She moved to sit beside Blake's mother. Touching Giulia's hand, she said, "I understand. It's a challenging time for her. And I'm still very much a stranger."

Giulia quickly denied the assertion. "You're already one of us, sweetie." She patted her hands. "I've never seen my son happier. And that's because of you."

Krista beamed at the statement. "Blake has been good for me as well. He's taken me out of my shell, encouraged me to experience new things."

She'd undergone a transformation in Boracay, both in the physical sense and in mindset. Her friends might have given her the initial push with their attempts at a makeover, but it had ultimately been Krista's decision to take chances and live her life to the fullest. Blake's love for her had boosted the ever-growing confidence she had in herself.

"Speaking of whom, where is the darling boy?"

Sean answered. "He said he'd check the blood donation process. He should be back soon."

Krista turned in the direction she'd last seen Blake. Sure enough, he was approaching from the area marked "Blood Bank." He wore a scowl, a rare sight these days.

"What's wrong?" Krista asked when he slumped beside her.

"They're not open until eight. The service desk was empty, and nobody knew anything about options other than wait," he replied, brusque. "We have to sit on our asses while Uncle Jack fights for his life." His hand clenched.

Krista eyed the wall clock. Quarter to five. Her body craved sleep, but she was needed here. And she wanted to know more about Jack O'Connor. She had a feeling he'd lead her to her biological father.

Her gaze shifted to Blake's parents. Giulia's head nestled on Sean's shoulder. *So sweet.* They looked exhausted, though. Dark rings shadowed both sets of eyes, and both had skin that was pale and lined with worry. She turned to Blake, but he was already talking to his parents.

"Da, Ma, you should go home, get some rest. Krista and I will wait here for Aidan and Ronan and keep *Tita* Belen company." He held Krista's hand. "We'll help out at the pub tonight, is that okay with you, sweetheart?"

"Yes, of course." Her smile encompassed all three Ryans.

Sean tipped his head in acknowledgment of the suggestion and stood, holding out his hand to assist his wife to her feet. Blake did the same for Krista.

"Give Belen a hug from us, and call us if there's news, sweetie," Giulia told her son after embracing them both. "Try to get some rest while you wait." She looked around the room, at a woman retching by the trash can, and grimaced. After another gentle pat on Krista's arm, she left with her husband.

CHAPTER FIVE

Upper West Side

Blake observed Krista as they returned to their seats. Pink tinted her cheeks, and light brightened her eyes. He shook off his frustration over the blood donation and asked, "What got you excited?"

Krista grabbed his hands and squeezed them. "Honey, your Uncle Jack was based in Clark in the mid-to-late eighties. Da told me."

Blake blinked, surprised. That was, indeed, important information. Marissa Lopez had spent a single night with an American airman who saved her from would-be rapists. Krista was the result of that sexual encounter.

The officer disappeared in the middle of the night, while Krista's mother was sleeping in her small apartment where she'd taken him to tend to his wounds. Marissa had looked for her lover when she realized she was pregnant but didn't find him.

Without access to the base, Krista's mother had had to wait for John to visit the restaurant where she worked. He never showed, making her think he'd either been deployed, re-assigned, or worse, had been killed in the line of duty. She'd left town before her condition became noticeable. If John was still alive and had returned to Clark, Krista's mom wouldn't have known it.

"I also heard Mrs. O'Connor refer to her husband as John."

Blake had noticed that, too. It held no significance to him, so he'd dismissed it as something intimate shared between husband and wife. To Krista, it meant something else.

"So, Uncle Jack was in the US Air Force, assigned to Clark around the time you were conceived, the two of you have the same blood type, and he is also named John," he recited the possible evidence. Krista's hopeful face reflected the inference she'd made. "Are you thinking he might be your biological father?" he asked, allowing his skepticism to show in his voice.

Her forehead creased. "My first thought was your Uncle Jack could know John, might have served with him. But the more I've learned, the more I think they could be the same person. My mom is O negative. I could only have gotten the B negative from my birth father." She shook their joined hands. "Blake, those are the only clues I have. For them to line up so perfectly is more than just a coincidence, don't you think?"

She'd never indicated a desire to look for her father until now. What little information she'd gathered had Krista reaching the conclusion she desired the most: for Jack to be John. But that would be too easy, too convenient.

As much as he understood her desire to get some answers to questions about her identity and heritage, he wanted her to exercise caution. He feared that her hopes would be dashed, that her heart might be broken.

Looking at his beloved's face, he couldn't bring himself to dampen her optimism by airing his doubts. He'd be unhappy if he was responsible for Krista's misery. He didn't want their Christmas to be blue.

Blake brought her closer for a hug. "You're right: it does all align. Unfortunately, we'll have to wait to get any more concrete proof."

She laid her head on his shoulder. "Do they live far?"

"Who?"

She straightened and peered at him as if she thought her change of subject shouldn't have confused him. "Ma and Da, where do they stay?"

"They have a brownstone in the Upper West Side. It's been in Da's family since his parents arrived in the twenties. I didn't want to overwhelm you on your first meeting with my parents; that's why I booked us a room at The Plaza rather than stay with them."

"Oh. Of course. Thanks." With a wave of her hand, she accepted his explanation. It paused mid-air as if she'd taken back the dismissal. "Wait, is there something in the house you don't want me to see?"

Blake groaned. "My mom still has all my childhood mementos displayed all over the place. All of ours, particularly Aidan's. Mr. Over-Achiever's medals and trophies could fetch a tidy sum at the pawnshop if our parents ever needed funds." He kissed her forehead. "I don't want you to be so impressed with all his accolades that you'll throw me over for him."

She made a cute face, her nose scrunching up. "Not gonna happen. He won't pass with my parents. Certainly not with my mom."

Blake was only joking when he'd said it, but relief filled him at her preference for him over his brother. In the past, he'd always lost to Aidan, whether with girls or competitions.

"I think I'll keep you even if you only got participation trophies." Krista winked at him. "Oh, and Maddie would kill me," she added, her eyes gleaming with humor at the mention of her best friend.

"Why would the lovely Ms. Duvall kill you? Did you scold her for arriving late to a meeting?"

Krista jumped up with a squeal at the unexpected question behind her. Blake stood too, happy that his older brother had finally arrived.

"Aidan. It's great to see you. How have you been?" Krista accepted a hug, delight in seeing somebody she knew evident in her wide smile.

"Doing fine. Until today."

Blake could have kicked him for erasing Krista's good humor. She paled again at the curt reminder of where they were and the reason behind their presence there: Uncle Jack. He stepped closer to Krista and held her hand.

"Did you and Ronan get the scum who put Uncle Jack on the operating table?" He had every confidence in Aidan, a lieutenant colonel in the US Air Force, and their friend, a detective with the New York Police Department. Nobody messed with their family and got away with it.

"Yes." Disgust laced Aidan's voice. "We had to double back, but we eventually found him. He was so high, he didn't get far from the pub. It looked like Uncle Jack got a few licks in before the fucker stabbed him. Sorry, Krista." He added the last when she visibly winced at the harsh language.

"It's fine. I've heard worse." She waved dismissively before sitting back down.

Blake smiled at the blatant lie. Growing up in a provincial town far from the big city, with a schoolteacher for an adoptive father, Krista had had a genteel and sheltered upbringing. The worst curse she'd ever said in his presence was "shit," and even that she'd only uttered under her breath.

"Where's the perp now?" He inclined his head, signaling his brother to move out of Krista's hearing.

"At Midtown South. Ronan's partner made the arrest."

By the book. He'd thought so. Being the victim's son, Ronan couldn't be the arresting officer. "Did he resist?"

"Yeah."

The unholy glee in the one-word answer told the tale. Jack O'Connor's son was able to exact a measure of revenge against the man who had stabbed his father. Blake bumped fists with Aidan.

"Speaking of Ro— There he is." Blake stepped forward to exchange back slaps with his friend. His weary and much-too-lean friend.

"Thanks for being here," Ronan said. "You didn't have to come. You couldn't have gotten more than a couple hours of sleep. Aidan said you only arrived last night."

"Not a bother. Family comes first."

"Appreciate it, Blake. Mom and Dad do too, I'm sure." He scrubbed a hand over his face as if to wipe off the fleeting expression of vulnerability he'd exposed at the mention of his father. "Heard you got yourself caught," he said after a few seconds of awkward silence.

Blake grinned. "I did. She's here. I'll introduce you."

"For real?" Ronan craned his neck to see around him. Blake turned aside to give him a clear view.

Ronan's eyebrows met in the middle when he caught sight of Krista. "She's mixed," he said without inflection.

If the tone had been insulting, Blake would have taken Ronan to task. As it was merely a statement of fact, he let it go. After all, Ronan was of mixed race, too.

Krista had risen to her feet as she saw them approach. Blake curled his arm around his girlfriend's waist when he reached her side. She met Ronan's fixed gaze steadily.

"Krista, I'd like you to meet Ronan O'Connor. Ronan, Krista Lopez."

Blake watched Krista closely while he made the introduction. Her eyes widened when she heard Ronan's last name.

"*Magandang umaga*, Krista. I'm pleased to meet you." Ronan greeted her "Good morning," in Filipino. He extended his hand.

Krista's lips curved, showing her delight in hearing her native language spoken. She accepted Ronan's handshake graciously. "It's nice to meet you too, Ronan. I wish the circumstances were better. I'm praying for your dad's quick recovery."

Ronan stared at Krista's face intently before responding with a simple, "Thank you."

A buzzing sound came from the direction of Ronan's back pocket. He pulled his hand from Krista's clasp to reach for it. Without looking at it, he pressed a thumb to silence the vibration. He addressed all three of them but took another lingering look at Krista. "I gotta go. Duty calls. See you at the pub later."

CHAPTER SIX

Times Square

Beside Krista, her boyfriend muttered, "When did he grow up?" almost to himself. They'd sat back down after Ronan left. Except for Aidan. He leaned against the wall in the space between two rows of chairs.

Meeting Jack O'Connor's son had been ... interesting. She hadn't known what to expect from him after his mother's coldness. He wasn't warm, but he wasn't antagonistic, either. He kept looking at her mouth. What was that about?

"How are you doing, love?" Blake inquired, noticing her silence.

"I'm fine. Resting," Krista replied. "Is he a cop, Ronan?" He looked like the ones she occasionally saw on TV. Leather jacket, longish hair, stubble, flat eyes, world-weary air. He looked anywhere from twenty-five to twenty-eight years old. Like his mother, he had a serious disposition. Ronan resembled Belen O'Connor in everything but height. With Krista's boots on, they were both six feet tall.

"Yeah. He graduated from the academy right before I left for the Philippines. I've only seen him a couple of times since, when I came home for Christmas. Usually just on our birthdays."

"Whose? Yours and Ronan's?"

"No, sweetheart. *Tita* Belen's and mine. Like you two." Blake glanced between her and his brother. "Her real birthday is the 25th, but because of the time difference, she celebrates it here on the Eve, same as me. It's been our families' tradition to close the pub early and have a combined *céili* and *noche buena*."

"Oh, of course. *Belen* in Tagalog means the nativity. Duh." Krista slapped a hand on her forehead. "Sorry."

He dismissed the apology with a squeeze of her hand.

In their nearly-two-month relationship, they had often talked about their immediate families: her parents and two siblings, Farrah and Alex; and his parents, and Aidan, Craig, and Darcy. He'd mentioned the O'Connors often, but not in detail. Even if he had, the other family simply hadn't registered with her. She wished now she'd paid more attention.

"We'll keep it low-key this year."

"Probably for the best. We don't know what Uncle Jack's condition will be in two days," Aidan said, moving to sit beside Krista.

A new group had spilled into the waiting room. Literally. The men were falling on their butts on the floor, cursing and laughing uproariously. The women, in glittery short dresses showing underneath faux-fur coats, were slip-sliding in their towering stilettoes. Even from several feet away, the unpleasant mix of cheap perfume and copious amounts of alcohol reeked from them.

Krista returned her attention to the Ryan brothers who were talking over her head.

"Why do you say that? What'd you learn?" Blake asked his brother. "*Tita* Belen hasn't come back from the CCU, so we don't have an update yet."

"Nothing new. Still in a coma. Heard the blood loss was severe. They've been giving him transfusions, but his response is slow," Aidan replied. "Ronan called *Tita* Belen while we were on the way here," he further explained when he saw their questioning looks.

Krista couldn't help herself. She blurted out, "Is there any way you can get the blood bank opened early? My blood is the same type as your uncle's. I'd like to donate, if it'll help wake him up."

"Baby, I already tried." Blake's tone held barely concealed pique.

Krista ignored him, keeping her gaze on Aidan. She'd soothe Blake's hurt pride later, after she had helped the man who could possibly be her biological father.

Aidan's eyes flicked from one to the other. After what seemed like hours, even though it was only a few seconds, he spoke. "I'll see what I can do." He stood and sauntered away to the west side of the building, in the opposite direction from the blood bank.

"He's going the wrong way," Krista observed, brows furrowed in confusion.

"No. He's going where I should have gone earlier: the hospital administration." Blake's scowl matched the one he wore when they'd fought over telling their officemates about their relationship. That time, like this one, her actions had irritated him. He clearly felt slighted that she had asked his brother to help where he had failed.

Krista touched his arm. "I'm sorry, hon. I just want—"

"I know. A lieutenant colonel in the Air Force has more clout than me, a mere CEO of a billion-dollar corporation. I get it."

The sharp bite in Blake's tone raised Krista's hackles. She balled her fists and scooted away. "I believe in maximizing all available resources, and your brother is a handy one right now."

"I already said I understood. There's no need to rub it in my face." Blake jumped to his feet and declared, "I'm gonna go grab some coffee. Are you okay until Aidan gets back?"

"I'll be fine. If you could bring me back some orange juice and a sandwich with eggs and spinach, I'd appreciate it. Thank you."

He grunted an acknowledgment of her order and left.

Krista could have gone with Blake, but his pissy mood annoyed her. Better to keep their distance until his temper cooled. She was usually the ill-tempered one in the morning before her first coffee, but today, her boyfriend rivaled her in grouchiness.

Her mind wandered back to Jack O'Connor. *Do I look like him?* They said girls oftentimes resembled their fathers more than their mothers. That was how everyone in their small town had come to the conclusion that Krista wasn't Arsenio Lopez's natural daughter. She stood almost a head taller than him, and her Anglo facial features looked nothing like his broad Malay-dominant countenance.

She took her cell phone from her bag. *Shit. Battery is dying already?* Krista had left the data roaming on since they left the hotel. It had been constantly looking for networks. *Ugh.* Her cell phone bill would be astronomical. Good thing she didn't have to pay rent on her best friend Maddie's condo, or else she'd be sacrificing one indulgence next month. Probably a new pair of shoes.

Krista went still. She didn't need more shoes. She just got new ones. Krista set her bag to the side, leaned back, and lifted her feet. Her Jimmy Choo-boots-clad feet. Two-freaking-thousand dollars. Blake had paid one hundred thousand pesos for a pair of over-the-knee boots. *Holy extravagance, Batman.*

"Those are gorgeous."

Krista dropped her feet with a thud. Face red, she lifted her gaze to the owner of the melodic voice that had paid her the compliment.

Talk about gorgeous. Tight black curls, flawless dark skin, high cheekbones, and gleaming toothpaste-commercial teeth showing between red lips, stretched wide in a friendly smile, comprised a stunning face. If that didn't stop traffic, the long-lashed blue eyes certainly would.

Krista must not have responded fast enough, because the glorious being in front of her stopped smiling and made a move to step away.

"Oh, thank you. I'm sorry. I was struck speechless. You're so ... beautiful." The woman looked like Vanessa Williams, only darker.

For some reason, Miss America took that as an invitation to take a seat beside Krista. "So are you." She crossed her legs, showing off the same boots in pale pink instead of Krista's black. "Samesies."

Delighted with the beautiful stranger's playfulness, Krista mirrored the pose with the opposite leg and said, "Twinning!"

They both laughed in shared camaraderie known to women all over the world, no matter where they came from.

"Hi, I'm Krista," she said, holding out her hand.

The other woman shook it enthusiastically. "I'm—"

"Summer, what are you doing here?"

"Aidan? Aidan Ryan? Oh, my gosh! It's great to see you." Summer rushed to enfold him in a hug.

While Summer exuded warmth and excitement upon seeing an old friend, Aidan held himself stiff in her embrace. He stepped back to extricate himself from her arms. Frosty blue-gray eyes met confused baby blues.

"Darling, really? Are you still mad at me? It's been what? Nineteen years?" She reached up to touch Aidan's face. Unlike Krista, Summer needed every bit of the boots' four-inch heels to give her height. Even wearing them, she stood a head shorter than the military officer.

"I was a child. A spoiled, bratty, selfish infant who had abandonment issues. I wanted to hurt you before you could leave me. I'm sorry. Please forgive me."

Krista leaned forward in her seat, enthralled by the drama unfolding before her. She didn't know what Summer had done to Aidan nearly two decades ago, but if she were him, Krista would forgive her based on that apology alone. The intensity in the other woman's voice and the plea in her eyes convinced Krista of her sincerity.

It must have registered with Aidan as well because he grasped the hand touching his face and lowered it. "Fine, you're forgiven."

Summer squealed happily and threw her arms around him once more. "Thank you, handsome. Come, let's sit beside my new friend and I'll tell you." She held onto Aidan's arm and tugged him towards Krista.

Aidan caught Krista's gaze and lifted a brow in inquiry. She stood and lifted her shoulders in a shrug, unsure what he'd asked her. She couldn't read brow language well, unless the brows were raised by Blake or Maddie.

Maddie! She'd forgotten Maddie, her best friend who had a crush on Aidan. She should have been angrier at this stunning woman's touchy-feely ways with her friend's object of admiration, but oddly she wasn't. Summer was too charming. And married, if the rings adorning her left hand were any indication.

"Aidan, this beautiful—and goodness, quite tall—young lady is Krista."

"I know." Aidan's voice barely concealed his laughter.

"You know? How did you know?" Summer turned back to Aidan in surprise.

"Krista is my brother's girlfriend."

"Which brother?" Summer faced Krista, the red tone of her skin becoming more pronounced.

"The middle one. I'm dating Blake."

"Blake. Oh dear, I guess I should apologize to him too, huh?" Summer plopped herself down on the chair and buried her face in her hands with a dramatic groan.

Krista remained standing. She needed to stretch her legs and give her butt a rest from the rigid plastic.

Aidan returned to his favorite spot against the wall. "If you feel you have to."

Summer looked up. "I want to. Where is he, anyway? Oh my God! Is he why you're in the hospital? Is he sick? Has he been in an accident?" Summer threw the rapid-fire questions to both Krista and Aidan, her gaze swinging wildly between them.

Why she felt she had to reassure the other woman of Blake's good health, Krista didn't know, but she stooped down and patted Summer on the shoulder.

"He's fine. He just went to get coffee." She straightened, sensing Blake's presence nearby. "In fact, here he is now."

CHAPTER SEVEN
Broadway

Blake came to a halt at the sight of Krista, Aidan, and another woman who looked vaguely familiar. His breath caught when she looked up and, with tears in her eyes, asked the others a string of questions. Only one woman in his acquaintance had brilliant-blue eyes that contrasted vividly against dark skin—Summer Maguire, Aidan's ex-girlfriend, Blake's first lover.

What the hell is she doing here? And why is Krista so chummy with her? With his eyes on his girlfriend, Blake approached the group. He stopped in front of Krista and kissed her on the lips, wanting to put on a united front.

He passed the coffee tray to Krista and faced the blast from his and Aidan's past. "Hello, Summer. Long time no see."

"Blake Ryan. All grown up." She held out both arms to him. "Can I get a hug?"

The look he threw his brother's way was met with an indifferent shrug. Asshole was having a laugh at his expense.

"Uh, sure," he said, standing still while the tiny beauty attempted to wrap her arms around him without success. She finally quit trying and just patted his sides.

"So, Blake. Uhm ... Can we please sit? I'm getting a crick in my neck looking up at all of you giants."

Blake allowed Summer to pull him down, and he took a seat beside her. He accepted his coffee from Krista, who had sat down to eat her breakfast the moment he handed it to her. *She's starving.* A twinge of guilt pierced him. He'd been doing a piss-poor job of taking care of her in his hometown.

"I'm sorry," Summer blurted out beside him, bringing his attention back to her.

"For what?" As soon as he said it, he knew. Before he could stop her, Summer was already babbling out her apologies.

"For using you to get back at Aidan. For seducing you when you were so young."

Fuuuuck!

Krista stared at them, slack-jawed, her sandwich perched on her lap, half-eaten. "You two were lovers?" she choked out. She glanced between Summer and Aidan with dawning horror, putting two and two together and arriving at the right answer.

Blake winced. He realized how sordid it all seemed—two brothers, one girl—especially to someone who had held onto her virginity until the age of thirty.

Summer practically pushed Blake to the floor in her rush to get to Krista. "Oh, babe. It wasn't their fault. Especially Blake. I was to blame," she explained to his astonished girlfriend. "Aidan wouldn't do what I wanted, so I used his brother to get back at him. I sneaked into Blake's bedroom and made sure Aidan would find us together."

Blake felt his face turn crimson. "Summer, it's okay. Apology accepted. No need to get into details."

Summer waved an imperious hand and continued her story. "I didn't plan on anything to happen, but, well ... one thing led to another and ..."

"And?" Krista urged.

"And nothing. That's enough, Summer. This is neither the time nor the place to rehash ancient personal history." Aidan's steely command brooked no argument.

Chastened, Summer slapped a hand over her mouth. Krista moved one seat away, separating herself physically from the three Americans.

Blake scanned the hallway for unusual interest in their odd little group but found others preoccupied with their own business. The bunch of partygoers to his right were sprawled on the floor, playing cards. Nurses and hospital staff went about their work, oblivious to their drama on this side of the waiting room.

Whew. God bless indifferent New Yorkers. He didn't care to be featured on YouTube with a salacious version of something that hormonal teenagers went through every day, all over America. Possibly not in the Philippines, where the Catholics practiced their faith zealously, but it was perfectly normal in the US. He hoped Krista understood that.

Blake snuck a glance at her. She sat hunched on the chair with her chin resting on a closed right fist, elbow braced on knee, teeth biting down on her bottom lip.

Just as he thought of going to her, Krista dropped her arm to her lap and straightened her spine. She glanced at him before raising her gaze to Aidan. "What did you find out about the blood donation?"

"The hospital has stored blood for emergencies. If they run out, they'll call the Red Cross. But, if there are family members present, willing to give blood, they will accept the donation, even outside office hours. The operative word is 'family.' We consider Uncle Jack family, but we're not actually related. We'll have to wait until the blood bank opens at eight. I apologize for not telling you sooner."

Krista's mouth turned down in disappointment. "Thanks for checking."

"Uncle Jack? Jack O'Connor? From the pub? He's why you're all here?" Summer piped up.

Blake had forgotten that Summer's father was Irish, too. The Ryan O'Connor Pub and Restaurant was a favorite haunt among their parents' generation. Along with her beauty, their shared heritage had made her attractive to Aidan and him when they were younger. "Yes. He was stabbed outside the pub in a thwarted robbery earlier this morning."

"Wait. My partner operated on a stabbing victim a few hours ago," Summer announced. "That's why I'm here. To drag Sam home." She turned to Krista. "I was about to do that when I saw you and got distracted. Maybe a surgeon will be able to facilitate the process for you. I'll have Sam paged now. Be right back." Without waiting for a response, she got to her feet and took off for the nurse's station.

No one spoke. They all watched Summer's disappearing form. When she was out of sight, Krista finally turned around to face the brothers. She huffed out a rueful breath. "Well."

"Yeah, our Summer is a force of nature." Aidan sat beside Blake and dropped a bombshell in a quiet voice. "I never slept with her."

The fuck? Blake squinted at his brother. Aidan never lied. He would keep his mouth shut rather than say something untrue. "You guys were together all through high school. You were always kissing and touching in public."

"All for show. We were each other's cover. I wanted to concentrate on my studies, graduate early. I didn't need the distraction of girls to derail my plans. She needed me to keep the boys away from her."

"Are you saying that night was her first time, too?"

"Maybe. Possibly. I didn't want to be her experiment, so she turned to you."

"That's messed up, Aidan. I didn't know what I was doing. I could have hurt her."

"*She* could have hurt *you*. Why do you think I split from her?"

"Because you're an ass?" Blake teased.

"True. But also because you had a crush on her. And she would have only broken your heart."

"How did you know that, Oh Wise One? You have superpowers I don't know about?"

"That's how," Aidan replied, inclining his head to the left.

To Summer returning to them with her arm around the waist of a white-coated doctor.

Both men got to their feet to meet the newcomer. Krista was slower to rise. Blake briefly saw her gape at the pair before composing her features.

"Guys! I didn't have to page her. She was already coming out. This is Dr. Samantha Vasquez, my wife. Sam, meet the lovely Krista. *Aaand*, the Ryan brothers, Aidan and Blake," Summer said, introducing them with a flourish.

With twinkling eyes, Dr. Vasquez shook their proffered hands. "*The* Ryan brothers from high school?" she teased her wife.

"Yes. All is forgiven and forgotten. We're all fine." She waved her hands in the air, dismissing the topic. "Krista here needs your help. Tell her, babe."

"I want to donate blood to Jack O'Connor. I was informed we have the same type."

"Are you related to the patient?"

Krista reached for Blake's hand. "Uhm, there's a slim possibility."

The doctor stared at Krista without speaking for a few seconds. Krista's grip on her boyfriend's hand tightened while they waited for Sam's decision.

"All right. I'll get a nurse to assist you. The process may take a couple of hours. We need to screen you for HIV, hep B, etcetera. Follow me."

"I'm going with you," Blake asserted.

"I'll stay here. Make sure *Tita* Belen has company," Aidan said.

Blake nodded to his girlfriend, wordlessly telling her to go ahead.

"Don't mention to *Tita* Belen that Krista is donating blood for Uncle Jack," he told his brother.

"Okay. If I'm not here when you're finished, I'll see you at the pub."

"Yup. All hands on deck tonight. Bye."

CHAPTER EIGHT

The Big Apple

Krista pressed the fingers of her right hand against the dressing the phlebotomist had put over the inside of her elbow. She waited for him to leave so she could talk to Blake. They were told to stay there for thirty minutes. She decided it would be a good use of their time to clear the air.

Blake must have read her thoughts. "Sweetheart, I'm sorry for snapping at you when you asked for Aidan's help earlier." He laced his fingers through hers. "I wanted to be the one doing things for you, not my brother. It frustrates me when he can deliver where I can't."

Krista's eyes softened. Being the eldest child herself, she'd felt an affinity for Aidan. She knew right away that he'd get things done. Not because she thought Blake couldn't accomplish the same, but because Aidan had the more arrogant aura. Where Blake used charm, Aidan used intimidation. Blake's way suited the Filipinos, Aidan's wouldn't. The military officer fitted Singapore, his current base, perfectly.

"Hon, you don't have to provide for me every time. Let others share in the giving. Let *me* give to *you* sometimes. I might not have as much money, but I can give you my time and my heart." She raised their joined hands to her lips and kissed his knuckles.

"And I appreciate that, love." Blake dropped a kiss on her lips. "If I'm out of sorts, it's because of Uncle Jack being stabbed and because of New York." He took a deep breath. "Do you know the saying 'you can never go home again' and what it means?" Blake waited for Krista's nod before he continued. "Don't get me wrong. I love New York. It's the greatest city in the world. I was born here. I grew up here. I'm proud to be able to call it my hometown."

Blake's fingers closed firmly over Krista's.

"But in New York, I'm always my parents' child, first. I'm always the second Ryan son. I'm always Aidan's younger brother. My accomplishments are nothing to those who know me here."

Blake's shoulders slumped, and a bitter smile shaped his lips.

"Increased your company's profit by five hundred percent, you say? That's nothing. Aidan almost died in Afghanistan when an IED exploded beside his truck. Patrick won the Ryder Cup for the US team. Ronan saved a child's life by rescuing her from druggie parents. Craig won a James Beard Award and two Michelin stars. Darcy has two master's degrees and is a PhD candidate. All at the ripe old age of twenty-four."

Krista's throat clogged from holding back her tears. She didn't want Blake to think she pitied him. No wonder he loved it in the Philippines. There, he was celebrated, respected, admired. In her country, her boyfriend was supremely confident; he managed everything and everybody around him.

She swallowed past the lump in her throat. "Honey, you're the best man I know. You provide a livelihood to thousands of Filipinos. Those profits you mentioned ensure the company will continue to stay in my country for a long time, helping the economy."

Krista's voice kept getting firmer as she extolled Blake's virtues. "I love you, and I'm proud of you. I'm sure your parents are, too."

Blake caressed her cheek. "I don't know what I did to deserve you, but I'm thankful I have you in my life." He planted a soft kiss on her lips. "I'm sorry for getting maudlin and making everything about me. Summer must have rubbed off some of her drama queen tendencies on me when she gave me a hug."

Krista spluttered a laugh. "Oh my God. I've never met anybody like her in my life."

Blake grimaced. "Yeah, she's a character, all right. She made a big show of blaming Aidan for driving her to my bed. She didn't want him to join the Air Force and leave her. I don't know how arranging for Aidan to find her with me would have stopped him. I can't pretend to understand how her brain works, so I won't even try."

Amusement still curling Krista's lips, she asked, "She popped your cherry?"

"Aargh! Yes. She might have just wanted to pretend we were in bed together, but she was naked. I was young and horny. I didn't even know how to put on a condom. I had enough presence of mind to pull out and spill on my bedsheets when I came. I don't remember a lot about that day, but I know it only took five minutes."

Her boyfriend's disgruntled expression was so adorable, Krista had to tease him. "Good thing you've learned a thing or two since then."

Blake bared his teeth. "Remind me to kick Aidan's ass when I see him next. It was all his fault."

Krista laughed out loud. "I'll hold him down for you."

Blake started laughing too.

Their joy in each other's company was like a balm to their tired souls. They'd only been in New York for twelve hours, and yet so much had happened already. The thought of what was still ahead sobered her right away.

Blake sensed her disquiet and ceased laughing as well. "What is it, love? Are you thinking of Uncle Jack again?"

"Yes. I want him to wake up already. I want him to get better."

"The hospital won't be able to transfuse him with your blood for many hours yet. Maybe even days."

They were told the steps that had to be taken - typing, separating, testing for various diseases, and labeling, all before it would reach Jack O'Connor. Dr. Vasquez could only expedite things so much for them.

The processes had to be completed in the proper manner.

"I know. I wish there was something we could do while we wait." Krista heaved a sigh.

"Maybe we can ask Aidan to check Uncle Jack's service records. Narrow down the dates when he was in Clark."

"It'll be great if he can do that. Can he?"

"I'm sure he'll find a way. If not, we can ask Ronan to investigate. That's his job, after all."

Ronan hadn't given her the death-stare like his mother had, so perhaps Blake was correct in that he might be willing to help.

"Can't hurt to try."

Krista laid her head on Blake's shoulder. *Will I know if he is my father when I see him?* They called it "*lukso ng dugo*" in the Philippines. Literally translated to "blood leap," it described a strange feeling of emotional attachment to someone, especially during the initial encounter. She couldn't wait to find out.

CHAPTER NINE
Hell's Kitchen

The interior of the Ryan O'Connor Pub and Restaurant did not look like any Irish pub Krista had ever seen. Not that she had been to many.

She dropped her purse on the bar before removing her coat and hopping onto a barstool. She swiveled around as she took in Blake's family business.

At two in the afternoon, still a couple of hours until it opened for the day, the pub was empty of customers and employees. From Krista's perch, she had an unobstructed view of the entire dining area.

The usual Irish symbols—shamrocks, Celtic crosses, Guinness beer, and whiskey—amply represented the business partners Sean and Jack's shared heritage. So did the green and white Christmas tinsel decorating the bar.

What surprised Krista were the individual touches showcasing the wives' heritages as well. Giulia's Italian roots likely influenced the family-style arrangements of the tables and chairs, with real tablecloths and napkins in reds, whites, and greens. Same with the bottles of wine, including the popular Moscato, Chianti, and Prosecco, on a mirrored wall.

Krista's gaze found the stage with its live band setup: drums, microphone stands, speakers, red and blue banners, and most importantly, a large TV monitor. The pub did *karaoke*. She instantly felt at home. Filipinos were known all over the world for their singing talent, and the fact that it was acknowledged here endeared her boyfriend's family to her even more.

She grinned at Blake, who'd been waiting patiently for her verdict. "I love it." Swinging her gaze to the far wall, she tipped her chin to a framed picture, one of several stunning landscapes of Ireland, Italy, and the Philippines.

"'Specially that one." In the photo, a rope hammock hung between coconut trees on a white sandy beach. The blue-green waters of the sea mirrored the aqua of the cloudless sky.

Krista had been on that exact hammock, on that specific beach, nearly two months ago. She knew without stepping closer to it what the caption would read: "Perlas, Boracay Island, Philippines." Blake's resort. Where she had fulfilled her Turning-Thirty Vow. Where she had declared "Seize the day" and fell in love.

She sank into Blake's embrace and tilted her head when he nuzzled her neck. "Do you miss it? We'll go back in March, during Holy Week," he said as he brushed his mouth against her ear. His warm breath stirred the fine hair around it, making her tremble.

"I'd like that." Krista's voice was barely a whisper. As always, Blake's mouth wreaked havoc on her senses; she didn't know what she'd just promised. She wanted his lips on hers, not on her neck, or her collar, or her chin. Impatient, she tugged at his hair to still his movement and pressed her lips to his.

It started sweet, a mere touch of soft flesh. Then Krista parted her lips at the same time his tongue sought entry. Any lingering coldness she felt melted as they sipped at each other. While snow chilled the streets of Midtown Manhattan, fire burned inside the multinational pub of Ryan O'Connor.

"My eyes! My virgin eyes. Get a room, yo."

The teasing voice broke through their sensual haze. Krista unwrapped her legs from Blake's hips. He stiffened but didn't let her go; he just lifted his lips away and muttered under his breath, "At this rate, I'm not going to have any brothers left. I'mma kill this one, too."

Krista giggled and buried her burning face against his chest. Beneath her cheeks she felt the double-time beat of his heart. She looked down at his front. Sure enough, the bulge of his erection strained the zipper covering it.

Poor guy. He wouldn't get relief anytime soon. After their return to the hotel from the hospital, they'd dived into bed and slept the rest of the morning. Five hours' sleep wasn't enough, but it was more than they'd had the night before.

Krista patted Blake's chest then leaned to her right to view the man who had interrupted their impromptu make-out session.

The speaker looked so much like his father, there could be no mistaking his identity: Craig, the youngest

Ryan brother. At six feet four inches, he was tall and wide. His body blocked the pub table behind him. Though a smile played about his lips, it didn't reach his denim-blue eyes. This wasn't the same man Krista had seen in Blake's family portrait, taken the year before.

Craig caught her staring and wiggled his fingers at her, making her blush again. Sad eyes, maybe, but virgin eyes, hardly. Her boyfriend's younger brother was too flirty for that to still be true at age thirty-two.

Blake stepped back, finally, and turned to greet his brother. The men exchanged bear hugs, Blake giving as good as he got from Craig, despite standing a couple of inches shorter and weighing several pounds less. Krista flinched at the sound of flesh getting slapped. Though it snowed outside, both brothers wore thin shirts. Blake, in his blue Henley long-sleeved shirt over black jeans, had taken off his jacket the moment they entered the pub.

Craig was even more casually dressed. His white muscle shirt showed off impressive pecs and abs; his jeans encased thighs the size of tree trunks. The man was built; pure muscle, no fat. With his long black hair tied back at his nape in a queue—thankfully not a manbun—beard, and deeply tanned skin, he could play a warrior on TV.

"Sweetheart, this puny creature is Craig. Little brother," they both grinned at the falsity of the claim, "my girlfriend, Krista. Mine. Stop ogling."

"Hello, Krista." Craig held out a scarred hand, but before Krista could shake it, he bent down and enveloped her in a hug.

"Hey, handshake only. Keep your paws to yourself." Her boyfriend pulled at his brother's arms to take them off her. They pretended to scuffle, throwing air punches that never connected, laughing their heads off the entire time.

Krista couldn't help but smile at their antics. She hadn't seen this side of Blake before. He kept a distance from their colleagues at the office. He played basketball and joked with them, but there was always the disparity of their positions between them.

She was also happy that the sadness that had clung to the youngest Ryan son when he first came in had gone.

"B!" A tiny ball of energy burst through the door and launched herself at Blake.

"D!" Her boyfriend caught the young woman mid-air and swung her about the room as if she was but a pillow. Brother and sister laughed in delight, their pleasure in each other's company punctuated by the tight embrace they shared.

Krista's heart swelled. Images of Blake playing with their daughter in exactly the same way filled her mind's eye.

She'd never had this. Her adoptive father, though he loved her, was not a playful man. They'd read books together, which had been fun in its own way. But it wasn't as exuberantly joyful as the Ryans' reunion.

"He'll be a wonderful father," Giulia remarked beside her.

Krista hopped down from the stool to greet the Ryan matriarch. Her cheeks red from the older woman's remark, she stammered, "Uh, we're not ... I'm not ... I'm on the pill."

Giulia's laughter shook her whole frame.

Krista buried her face in her palms, groaning in embarrassment.

Blake's mother patted her arm. "I'm glad you're being responsible. I'd love to have grandchildren, but not until you're both ready. Come, I'll introduce you to our youngest."

***

Blake watched as Krista bonded with his sister, their dark heads close together as they whispered and giggled.

"They're not talking about you, vain man. Move. The food will get cold." With a platter in each hand, Craig nudged Blake forward with his foot.

Blake set the food in the middle of the table, lifted Darcy out of the chair beside Krista, and deposited her on another.

"Hey!" His sister slapped his arm. "We were talking."

"Now you're not." He dropped a kiss on Krista's head before sitting on the chair his sister had involuntarily vacated.

"You're a bully, B." Darcy stuck out her tongue at him. She looked all of twelve when she did that. No one who saw her now would think she was a bona fide genius. Blake wasn't the only one who reverted to childhood when home in New York. His siblings did, too.

"Zip it, brat. Da is about to say grace." He crossed himself, then held hands with Darcy and Krista. Everyone did the same.

At the head of the table, Sean intoned, "Heavenly Father, we praise and thank you for the many blessings you have given us today. We are grateful for the gathering of our family, this circle of love and strength. We ask you to bless us and our food, and to bless those we love who are not with us today. We offer special prayers of healing for our brother, Jack. We ask these things in Jesus' name. Amen."

A chorus of amen filled the room.

"*Bímis ag ithe*. Let's eat."

"Not so fast," said Ma, and everyone groaned. "Craig, explain to Krista what you've prepared."

"Make it quick. I'm hungry," Aidan grumbled.

"*Hangry* more like," Blake whispered to Krista, who pinched his side to shush him. Her lips curved. He knew she remembered her excuse for her rudeness to him, the first day in Boracay.

"Since I'm taking over the kitchen for *Tita* Belen while they're at the hospital, I've cooked for you some of the restaurant's menu items so I can re-familiarize myself with them."

Craig's words reminded Blake that his brother had lived everywhere but New York for the past ten years. He resided in LA before he moved to Thailand. Before then, he'd been working for master chefs all over the world, from France to Italy to DC, never staying in one place for longer than a year.

"In front of you, Krista, is Guinness *caldereta,* our version of beef stew. There's steamed rice, of course. Or brown soda bread, if that's what you prefer. Next to that is *longganisa* coddle. Instead of regular bangers, we use the sweeter Filipino pork sausage. Lastly, we have chicken *lechon* with mushrooms and whiskey-cream sauce. Enjoy."

"Now, let's eat." Aidan was already reaching for the roasted chicken.

Nobody spoke for a while; only the sound of cutlery and requests to pass dishes could be heard, along with moans of satisfaction as the flavors exploded in their mouths. Blake glanced at Craig, amazed once again by his brother's talent.

"These are all delicious, Craig. Thank you for cooking all of these for us. *Salamat.*" Ever so gracious, Krista thanked his brother in Filipino.

"*Walang anuman,* Krista. It was my pleasure." Craig threw Blake a sly grin before saying, "Let me know if you want me to cook for your wedding, and I'll make sure to clear my calendar."

Blake didn't know whether he wanted to wring his brother's neck or thank him. He did want to ask Craig to cater their wedding dinner, whenever that may be. After he proposed to Krista.

"I'm the best man," Aidan declared. Autocratic jerk didn't even look up from his plate. Just issued the statement as if it were a done deal.

Krista coughed beside him. She was in the act of drinking water when his fool brothers decided to tag-team him.

"Nobody asked you. Maybe we'll elope." Hard fingers from his right caught a fleshy part in his side and twisted. "Aw!"

"Blake Henry Ryan, you will do no such thing," his mother yelled, getting to her feet to assert her authority. "Aidan Garrett, Craig Edward, stop baiting your brother. They will make plans when they see fit, and neither of you have any say in the matter. Are we clear?"

Ouch. Full names? There could only be one answer. "Yes, Ma," all three of them chorused. Their mother sat back down, satisfied that she'd laid down the law. Their Da, though he remained quiet, gave them all a warning glance.

Darcy snickered to his left. "Shut it, Darcy Elizabeth." Blake's mock scowl only increased her giggles.

"Once you're all done eating, here are your assignments for the evening: Aidan, bar; Blake, take care of the books; Craig, kitchen; Darcy, cash register;

Sean, your cronies will be here wanting an update on Jack—manage them. I'll be at my usual post, supervising the waitstaff. Are there any questions?" His mother, Generalissimo Ryan herself, at her most commanding.

"Where's Patrick?" Blake hadn't seen hide nor hair of Uncle Jack and *Tita* Belen's eldest son.

Darcy replied, "He just flew in from Indonesia. Said he'd go straight to the hospital as soon as the plane lands."

Blake's eyebrow rose. The response came too quickly. As if his sister was used to accounting for the golfer's whereabouts. He looked at Aidan across from him, who was also frowning at Darcy.

None of the Ryan boys were close to Patrick. It seemed their only sister was. Blake hoped it was only friendship and nothing more.

"Ronan's evening shift. He said he'll pass by before closing." Completing her report on the O'Connor brothers, Darcy went back to eating.

Blake huffed out a breath. Knowing about his little sister's friendship with Ronan relieved him. He could get behind *that* relationship. The other, not so much.

"May I have an assignment too?" Krista piped up.

"Of course, sweetie. What would you like to do?"

"After having tasted all this," she stretched a hand to indicate the nearly-empty dishes, "I want to help in the kitchen. I've cooked the Filipino version of some of these dishes at my parents' café before. I can help with the prep, if the chefs won't mind." She addressed the last to Craig, who nodded his agreement.

"You truly are a gem. My son is a lucky man." Giulia beamed at her.

Blake draped his arm over Krista's shoulder. "That, I am." He pressed a kiss on her forehead. For her ears only, he said, "I am, indeed, a lucky man. Thank you, love. I'm sorry we have to cancel *Hamilton* tonight."

"Don't be. I'm fine. I'd rather stay and help. I hope you received a refund."

"I don't care about that. I care more about you not having any fun in New York."

"We're only on our second day of our two-week vacation. I'm sure we'll have opportunities to go out later, when things are better with your Uncle Jack."

"I'll make sure we go out tomorrow. I promise."

"Okay. Let's play it by ear. I don't want to go far." She stood and started to gather the dirty dishes together, but he stopped her.

"No heavy lifting for twenty-four hours." Blake reminded her of the nurse's orders after her blood draw.

"I know, and I won't. I'm sure a couple of plates are not too heavy. I can manage those."

"All right, I'll be in the office if you need me. Don't let Craig work you too hard." He strode to the closed door to the left of the bar, on the opposite side to the kitchen.

CHAPTER TEN

Eighth Avenue.

"Great job, Krista." Crouching before her, Craig held his hand, palm out, for a low-five. Behind him, the staff went about putting the kitchen to rights. The banging of pots and pans was interspersed with laughter and teasing from the close-knit crew as they celebrated the end of a working day that saw no major mishaps. "If you ever want to leave the exciting world of finance and try cooking for a living, let me know. I've enjoyed working with you."

Krista gave the broad hand a limp tap. She leaned back on the chair she'd collapsed onto the moment Craig announced the completion of the final service—seven and a half hours after they'd opened—and shut her eyes.

"Thanks, but I don't think so. I have so much respect for you, my mom, and Mrs. O'Connor for doing this day in and day out. But this is a one-off thing. Tomorrow I'll help Blake with the books."

"What you see in that boring guy, I'll never know."

Krista opened her eyes to see Craig's teasing smile. "We like being boring together."

He took her hand again—the one with several band-aids covering nicks and cuts—and kissed the injured fingers. "You're pretty special. I'm glad I'm going to have you for a sister."

Awww. Though Blake hadn't proposed officially yet, his mention of elopement told her of his intentions. "Thank you, Craig. I'm happy to have two new brothers, too." She gave his cheek a kiss, then stretched her arms over her head. "Up."

She'd only wanted him to pull her to her feet, but he turned around and gestured to his back. "Hop on. I'll give you a ride."

Too used to being bigger than normal in her home country, Krista started to protest. Then she thought better of it. Compared to Craig, she *was* small. Wrapping her arms around his neck, Krista hopped on, her legs around his waist, for the first piggy-back ride of her life. "Giddyap. Yee-haw!"

Craig chuckled. "Wrong state, lass."

"Oops! Sorry." She dropped her chin to his shoulder and used it to nudge his ponytailed hair aside. "Hey, are you single? I've got this friend named Angela. She's always in Koh Samui. I'll introduce you to each other."

"Angela?" He paused in his stride across the pub. "Uhm, I'm actually not dating right now."

"Oh, I'm sorry. My gaydar is nonexistent. I didn't know you ... Whoa!" Krista nearly fell off his back. Craig laughed so hard, his shoulders shook with the rumble of his mirth.

"Put me down." When he obeyed, she demanded, "What's so funny?"

"I'm not gay."

"O ... kay? The way you said 'Angela,' I thought the idea of going out with a woman did not appeal."

"Not right now." His eyes turned bleak again. "My girlfriend just died last September. She was from Thailand. That's why I moved there." He bowed his head, hiding his grief.

She squeezed his arm. "I'm sorry for your loss."

"Thank you." He raised his chin, but kept his face averted. "Do you want to ride again?"

Not wanting to intrude further in his sorrow, she stepped back. "No, thank you. I can walk now."

Hands in his pockets, eyes fixed on the floor, he said, "I'm going back to the kitchen. Check if everything's put away properly. Tell my brothers I'll head home."

"Sorry to make you sad. See you tomorrow."

He lifted a hand to wave and left.

***

"How's the pub doing?" Aidan asked from his spot beside the window in the pub's office. Why he needed to stand there mystified Blake. It didn't look out to anything other than a dark alley. Unless he was checking to see if a vagrant sought shelter from the miserable weather in the narrow space. At close to midnight, with no moon in the sky and no street light reaching it, the alley was the perfect hiding place.

"Fine. Not much profit, but no massive losses, either." He reclined on the chair Uncle Jack usually occupied. His father's partner was the numbers guy, Da the ideas person. The oldest O'Connor kept a meticulous record. Blake had only needed to enter the previous night's receipts when he came in. He helped bus the tables once he'd done that, and he'd just closed the books on tonight's intake before Aidan entered.

The solvency of the pub relieved Blake of worry. With his investment in a resort in Boracay, he didn't have many assets to liquidate to help his parents if the pub had financial troubles. His other partners had been making noises about branching out in Palawan and in Quezon, the province where Krista's parents lived.

The reminder of Marissa and Arsenio Lopez had Blake massaging his temples.

"You okay?"

"Yeah, just a headache. It's been a hell of a day." They'd stopped service at the pub at ten, four hours earlier than normal for this season. After last night's incident, everyone was spooked and wanted the safety of hearth and home, especially his parents. Blake and his brothers had sent them and Darcy home as soon as the last customer left, with the promise to close the pub.

"I'm sorry I didn't tell you about Summer. It wasn't my secret to share." A rare admission of fault from his big brother. Surprising.

"I understand that. I'm relieved I wasn't the one who caused her to turn gay."

"Maybe you did. Sex with you was so bad, she swore off men forever." He guffawed.

Ass. Blake let Aidan laugh at his expense. He needed to share his dilemma with his confidant.

After a couple of minutes, Aidan's hilarity subsided.

Blake blurted out, "Krista thinks Uncle Jack might be her biological father."

"I guessed from her insistence on donating blood. What's your beef about it?" As if bracing for a long talk, Aidan adjusted his stance against the wall, leaning his frame fully onto it and crossing his arms in front of his chest.

"No beef. I support her one hundred percent. Just worried. It'll hurt a lot of people. Her parents, *Tita* Belen, Krista herself. She'll be devastated if he is and doesn't acknowledge her. Worse if he's not, because she's building her hopes around him. The fallout will be a mess."

"You're being overprotective. Krista is an intelligent, levelheaded woman. She's thirty, not eighteen."

"I know that, but she's letting her heart rule. She's *carpe diem*-ing the hell out of this."

"Didn't she do the same when she hooked up with you? You weren't exactly acceptable to her mother."

Ouch. Direct hit. He really shouldn't have told his brother everything. "That's different."

"It's not. She needs to know her roots. Both of you do. If you're going to marry her, you have to know her background for the sake of your future children."

We'll have beautiful children. Blake relaxed. Aidan made sense, as usual. "Not if, when."

"Have you proposed? I don't see a ring on her finger. You're doing it wrong, bro."

"Like you'd know anything about that."

"I don't. Who watched all the romcoms with Ma? You should know how to do this shit."

"Fuck off. I have a plan."

"Tell Krista, not me.

"I will. Soon. After this business about Uncle Jack is cleared up."

The door swung open.

"Where is she?" Patrick O'Connor barked. Heightened color matted his skin, and temper flashed in his brown eyes.

Blake got to his feet and moved to stand beside his brother. He mimicked Aidan's stance, crossing his arms in front of his chest.

"And a good evening to you too, Patrick. Who are you looking for?" Blake suspected the younger man sought Krista. Darcy said he'd planned to go to the hospital first. *Tita* Belen must have shared the reason for her antipathy for Krista with her older son.

"The b— The impostor. She made my mom cry." Patrick sounded like an overgrown brat.

Blake had to restrain himself from decking the younger man right there and then. His tone was clipped when he replied, "We don't know of any impostor around here."

"Blake, honey, can we go —"

Patrick blocked Krista's way in. "You! Mom said you're back and you've managed to con the Ryans into thinking you're someone else." He stabbed the air with his finger. "Well, Maire, too bad for you I lost my last tournament. You're not going to get a red cent out of me."

Krista's eyes bugged out and her mouth hung open. "What? First, I don't know who you are. Based on your attitude, I am not sorry you lost whatever tournament you're talking about. Second, this is my first time in the US, my name is Krista, and I've never pretended to be anybody else in my life."

That's my girl. Blake couldn't stop the smile that spread across his face. He'd seen this side of his girlfriend once, when she thought he'd deemed her unsuitable for Boracay. She was magnificent then, more so now.

"She's telling the truth, *Kuya* Patrick," Ronan said from behind Krista. "You should have talked to me before rushing over here, making accusations." He stepped forward to stand beside Krista, as if declaring his alliance with her. "You've never met Maire. I have. And I'm sure Mom did not use the word 'con' in referring to Krista."

Patrick kept his belligerent stance. If anything, he looked angrier now that he'd been scolded by his younger brother in front of a stranger. "How do you know she's telling the truth? Maybe she's more professional than Maire."

"Because she is who she says she is: Maria Krista Lopez, born on November 2nd, over thirty years ago in Pampanga to Marissa and Arsenio. Currently senior financial analyst at Blake's company."

"You ran a background check on my girlfriend?" Though he understood Ronan's motivation, he still felt mildly annoyed.

"She's clean," Aidan declared.

Blake scowled at his brother, who only lifted an eyebrow. Of course Aidan had run Krista. He worked in Intelligence. His approval of Krista as his future wife clearly stated his opinion of her trustworthiness.

"Look, can we sit? This is a long story, and I've already put in eight hours today." Ronan gestured to the chairs in front of the desk, asking Krista to precede him.

Blake held out his hand to his girlfriend. He *tsk*ed upon seeing the adhesive bandages on several of her fingers. She mouthed, "I'm fine," before sitting down and waiting for Ronan to explain.

CHAPTER ELEVEN
Hudson River

"I'll stand." The sullen announcement came from Ronan's older brother. He'd closed the door and leaned his shoulder against it.

Krista gave Patrick a side-eyed glance and tossed her hair, still fuming over his accusations. As if she'd ask for money from him. *Who the hell does he think he is?*

"I take it you met my mom this morning." Ronan sat opposite her on the other chair.

"Yes. She ... uhm..." She trailed off, unsure how to describe Belen's behavior towards her without offending the older woman's sons. The other was already mad at her.

"She gave you the cold shoulder. Was probably rude."

"A little bit," Krista admitted.

"I noticed that," Blake remarked from behind her. "Why did she freak when she saw Krista?"

Ronan rubbed the back of his neck before letting out a harsh breath. "A few years ago, a woman appeared at the pub claiming to be Dad's daughter. Called herself Maire. Said she was named after his maternal grandmother. Turned out to be a con job. She didn't bleed them dry, but the incident made them wary, particularly Mom. She must have thought it was happening all over again when she saw you. Another one of Dad's by-blows come to claim him."

Krista couldn't quite silence her gasp with her hand over her mouth. *Another? How many were there?*

"When did this happen?" Blake demanded.

"Right about the time Uncle Sean and Aunt Giulia went to visit you in the Philippines."

"Did my parents know?"

"Probably afterwards. When they got back. I don't think those four keep many secrets from one another."

Krista leaned forward. "How did they find out she was a fraud?"

"They didn't. I did. She'd been staying with them for a week already when I got back from training early. Caught her in my parents' room, trying to open the safe. Collared her right there and then."

"What was her sob story, and why did Uncle Jack believe her?" Aidan butted in.

"The usual crap. Drunken one-night stand. Apparently, Dad was a player when he was assigned to Clark. He was attracted to Filipinas, and they were attracted to him. Her mother was supposed to have been a server at a bar in Angeles City. Condom broke. When you sleep around a lot, there's always a possibility of that happening."

Krista's shoulders tensed. The story was alarmingly like her mother's.

"She showed a photo of Dad with his arms around her supposed mother; knew the names of the guys in the troop. There was a deathbed promise. Debts were allegedly owed for her to be able to come to the US to meet her biological father."

"Nothing original, but hard to disprove anything without going to the Philippines or contacting everyone in his old troop," Aidan observed.

"What did she look like? Why was it easy to convince your parents to fall in with her scheme?" Blake rubbed her back as he asked the question. Krista leaned into his touch, appreciating his unspoken support.

"It was obvious she was of mixed blood: Caucasian and Asian. Black hair, brown eyes. Taller than the typical Filipina. At first glance, she looked like us," he pointed to Patrick and himself, then at Krista, "but a closer look revealed some surgical work done."

"Why didn't your parents see that?" Krista asked, unable to hide her incredulity.

"They had always wanted a daughter. Mom miscarried a few times after me. It became dangerous for her to get pregnant, so she had her tubes tied. When this woman came along, the old wants returned. They were ready to give a twenty-seven-year-old orphan a home."

"What's the true story?" *Thirty-one now. Older than me.*

"It turned out most of what she claimed was true, except for the father. She'd found him a few years before. A vet who'd fallen on hard times, he was jealous of Dad's success. They saw *Kuya* Patrick's interview after he won a tournament in Ireland where he talked about his ties to the country, and they schemed to use the slight resemblance to their advantage."

"So it's my fault?" Patrick interrupted. "You didn't tell me this."

"Nobody is blaming you, and Mom didn't want you to know."

"How'd you get rid of her?" Aidan asked Ronan, steering the conversation back to the subject of the impostor.

"Had her declared an undesirable alien and deported. She can't ever come back to the US."

"Why did you think I was her if that was true?" Krista threw out at Patrick.

"As you heard, I didn't know all the details. Mom asked for money and I gave it. She's a proud woman, my mother. She doesn't ask for herself, but for others. Her so-called Filipino friends know she has a soft spot for them, and they take advantage all the time. I'm sick of it."

Patrick's voice had softened when he spoke of his mother, but his generalization of her compatriots raised Krista's hackles.

"Why didn't you ask for help? I live in the Philippines. I could have verified her story," Blake said.

Ronan lifted his shoulders. "There was no need. We dealt with the impostor. Whatever money she managed to steal from the pub was returned in full. Dad was ashamed about his past catching up with him. Mom was angry and sad at the same time. They just wanted to forget the whole thing happened."

Krista had heard enough. She stood to address the O'Connor brothers. "I'm not making any claim on your father." Only Blake knew her hopes and wants regarding Jack O'Connor. She doubted he'd told anybody else.

"When I met you this morning, I knew right away you were not Maire. But it made me think." Ronan got to his feet and leaned his hip on the desk.

Krista thought he looked like he was settling in for another story. She propped her head against Blake's shoulder. She was so tired. But Ronan seemed to have something important to say, so she decided to hear him out.

"For months after she left, I'd often wondered if we had another sibling out there in the Philippines. I'm sure Mom and Dad thought it, too. But nobody discussed the topic again. *Kuya* Patrick never cared about our Filipino roots—"

"Hey!" his brother protested.

"It's true, don't deny it." He sent a hard look in Patrick's direction before returning his attention to Krista. "I got assigned to a task force that kept me busy for years, and I forgot about looking for a brother or sister. Until you arrived this morning. You have a way of tilting your lips up on one side when you smile that reminded me of Dad." He paused as if he was waiting for that to sink in.

Krista straightened. Her pulse began to accelerate.

"That's why I ran a background check on you. I didn't find a lot of information except for your resume and business profile from your company website. I had to dig deeper to obtain your birth certificate. Like Aidan said, you're clean."

Aidan inclined his head in acknowledgment.

"However, I found a picture of you with your family in the Philippines on social media. You favor your mother—all three of you do. But the man who gave you his surname couldn't be your birth father. You don't look anything like him, and you're too tall to be his daughter. Your father would have to have been tall. He's probably white, same as him." Ronan pointed to the wall behind her.

Krista whirled around. So fast, Blake had to reach for her arms to steady her. Anger at Patrick had blinded her to everything else in the room when she came in. Now, in front of her were photos. Of Captain John Jackson O'Connor, according to the caption. *John. Jack.*

In his flight suit, standing beside a fighter jet, Jack O'Connor looked like Hollywood's ideal military hero. Tall, close-cropped black hair, twinkling eyes, the uptilt of his lips to one side that Ronan mentioned, Jack was confidence personified.

"He's a handsome devil, isn't he?" Ronan remarked beside her.

Krista nodded, hungrily taking in all the photos, her eyes darting from one to another. Sean Ryan was in some of the same pictures, but she only peered at Jack. One particular picture made her gasp: Jack with his troop, celebrating an event of some kind. They had their arms raised; some held champagne. Jack was in the foreground, smiling broadly. Above his right eye was a scar, a thin line that slashed his eyebrow. A scar that wasn't there in the flight suit picture but appeared in all the others, especially the later ones.

"Ronan, do you know how he got the scar?" Krista traced it with a trembling finger. Her heart in her mouth, she waited for the answer she yearned for.

"Dad said he got it in a fight with some thugs outside the base in the Philippines. One of them had a knife. He was happy he ducked in time. It only nicked him, otherwise he'd have gone blind."

"It needed stitches, but he insisted on taking me to safety first." Krista repeated the words her mother told her many years ago about her rescuer.

Tears falling from her eyes, she turned to Blake. "He's my father. He's John. I've found him."

Blake stepped closer and enfolded her in his arms. Krista clung to him, sobbing for reasons she couldn't identify. Relief, joy, uncertainty, and vindication all warred in her head and in her heart.

"It looks like you're making a claim on Dad after all." Ronan said gently.

"Yes, I am." Krista lifted her head from Blake's chest to face her father's—her father's! — two sons again. "My mother told me my father's name is John. He served in the US Air Force and was assigned to Clark in the late eighties. I also now know that we have the same blood type: B negative."

"Did you donate?" Ronan asked.

His voice raised, Patrick demanded, "Are you planning to tell my mom? I won't have you upsetting her more than you already did. Wait until Dad's better." He'd stepped closer to Krista.

Blake tightened his hold on her. "Be careful how you address Krista, Patrick. We all understand your love for your mother, but you're this close to disrespecting my girlfriend, and I won't allow that to happen. Do you understand me?"

Krista extended her hand wearily. "Guys, please. Don't fight."

The younger man backed away, muttering, "Sorry."

Krista dropped her hand. "I don't know what I'm going to do yet. I'm really tired. I want to rest now." Not waiting for a response, she turned her back on the others and leaned on her boyfriend.

Lifting her in his arms, Blake carried her to a chair and sat with her on his lap. Krista didn't stir when she heard the door close behind the other men. She slumped against his neck, and the rhythmic beat of his heart against her hand soothed her. This was fast becoming her favorite crying place. In Boracay, when she had told Blake about her mother and John, he'd held her like this.

John. She'd found her father. Her blood jumped when she saw his face for the first time. Just photos. She could only imagine how she'd feel if she met him in person. *Lukso ng dugo.*

"Do you think your *Tita* Belen will let me see him?"

"I don't know, baby. It depends on what the boys decide. If they tell her or wait until their dad wakes up. They might want to do a paternity test."

All of a sudden, fear gripped Krista. She straightened. "What if he doesn't wake up? What if he lost too much blood from his wounds? What if his body rejects my blood and he dies?"

"Baby, there's no use thinking about that. Let's hope for the best."

Krista's chest ached as she put into words her worst fears. "If he dies, I'll never know who my real father was. I'll never know where I came from." She'd lived in the Philippines all her life and had known the part of herself that was Filipino. But there was another part of her that had gone unexplored for thirty years. Until now.

He lifted a hand to tuck a lock of hair behind her ear. "You have a mother and a father who molded you, who love you. Why rely on someone who's a stranger to you to validate your identity?"

"You've always been secure in the knowledge of who you are from the time of your birth. With parents and siblings who resemble you. I didn't have that. I was the odd one most of my life. Half-Filipino, half-nothing. I didn't belong." Tears fell down her cheeks again. She let them flow. "I'm not asking them to love me. John, Belen, Patrick, and Ronan. They don't have to accept me. Meeting the man who helped create me will be enough. I won't be half-nothing anymore. I will be whole."

Blake brushed her tears away. "You don't have to demand love from anyone for them to give it to you. We may not be your blood, baby, but my family already loves you. With the Ryans, you already belong."

Krista sank back against his chest. Blake's statement invited no response. It was fact. She'd felt it all day long.

Deep inside, she felt shame. She'd lied. She did want at least one O'Connor to love her. The one who mattered most. Her father.

The door burst open. Ronan rushed in, his skin ashen. "*Ate* Krista, Blake, Mom just called. Dad convulsed and tore open his stitches. He's bleeding again. They took him back to surgery."

Krista sprang up and placed her hand on Ronan's arm. "What can we do?" Even as she asked, she knew there was only one thing she could do.

"Pray." Ronan took her hand in his. "Please pray for our dad, *Ate*." He withdrew his hand and nodded to Blake. "I'll call you as soon as we have an update on his condition."

CHAPTER TWELVE

St. Patrick's Cathedral

A single snowflake drifted away from the flurry that fell steadily from the sky. Shaped like a star, it fluttered close to the outer glass of the hotel's window before dancing back in the air, an invisible gust of wind controlling its graceful movement. Krista followed its descent until it disappeared.

How she envied the snowflake its lightness right now. To float without care, without the weight pressing down on her.

Two days before Christmas. Supposedly, the happiest season of all. It was usually her favorite holiday. Especially this year because of Blake's birthday; the first time they'd spend it together. Jack O'Connor's condition had postponed the celebration until he could attend.

Krista rubbed her eyes. They were gritty from her disturbed sleep. She'd tossed and turned all night. She'd prayed. She'd been tempted to ask her *barkada—M'amie,* her group of friends in the Philippines—to pray for him, too. But she didn't have confirmation of their relationship.

Yet.

In her heart, Krista knew. The man who had fathered her, the man her mother only knew as "John," was Jack O'Connor. She wanted to tell her *Nanay*, but it was too soon. She had to see him first. He had to call her his daughter first. For that to happen, he had to wake up.

If he ever did. Ronan had called at two in the morning to say his father had pulled through the surgery but remained unconscious. Even after that, her sleep had been fitful.

"What do you want to do today?" Blake asked from the bed.

They'd come back to their room after breakfast at the Food Hall, this time sampling sumptuous offerings from Épicerie Boulud and Lady M Cake Boutique. Replete from coffee, croissants, and slices of *mille crêpes*, they'd decided to take it easy before making their plans for the rest of the day. There was no rush to go to the hospital as long as Jack was still in a coma.

Krista turned from her spot at the window. "I want to stay close by," she replied, the "just in case" unspoken. "Let's keep to Midtown, if that's all right with you." She crossed the room and perched on the chaise at the foot of the bed.

"Central Park, The Met, Rockefeller Plaza, Broadway, that sort of thing?"

"Yes. Can we go to St. Patrick's Cathedral also? I want to say a prayer for ... um, your Uncle Jack."

Krista still didn't know what to call him. Not Mr. O'Connor, especially if they did DNA testing and it proved he was her biological father. Dad? Patrick and Ronan called him that. Maybe. If he asked.

Shaking her head, she returned her attention to Blake. "Is it reachable on foot? I've never seen snow in real life before coming here. I want to walk."

"Did we get you appropriate shoes? Your Nikes or your Jimmy Choos won't do."

"You're not buying me any more shoes," Krista said in exasperation. She swore, this man had a fetish for footwear. Hers, in particular. "Maddie loaned me a pair of snow boots. They'll do." She glared at Blake, daring him to disagree with her.

"Okay, okay. You're not Imelda." He rose from the bed, holding up both hands in mock surrender. "Jeez, one would think you're with me for love and not for my money and good looks." He sat beside her and nuzzled her neck.

"One would think," she gasped, her breath catching in her throat.

Here was lightness. Here, in Blake's arms, she could float. Be weightless. Be loved.

His right hand nudged aside the V-neck of her sweater, along with the strap of her bra. Every inch of her skin he bared received a kiss, a bite, a lick. The other hand crept beneath the soft material of the cashmere and swept across her back to unhook her bra, leaving heat in its wake. In a wink, her top came off.

"Blake, honey, what about sightseeing?" Her voice came out breathy, needy. She lay back on the bed; her spine couldn't hold her up. In that moment she knew what it meant to be boneless.

"I'm seeing some great sights down here." He'd pulled off her jeans and taken her panties along with them. "I'm looking at a garden with the most beautiful flower in full bloom, dew droplets clinging to its petals." He described the most feminine part of her as he spread her legs to kneel between them.

Krista liquified, hearing his words. Her blood heated as it coursed through her veins, and arousal dampened her thighs. She licked her lips. Moisture pooled beneath her tongue in anticipation of seeing his beautiful body bared, of tasting his skin, of kissing his mouth, and maybe, also his cock.

He was right. They needn't go out to see great sights. The ones in the hotel room couldn't be beat. No Greek statue at The Met could equal Blake in male beauty. No symphony at Carnegie Hall could match the music they'd make together with their moans and words of passion. Yes, truly, there was no better place in New York City than here.

***

Blake stretched and yawned. He'd finally gotten some sleep. They both had. Making love made them forget their troubles, at least for a short while.

He rolled onto his side to face Krista. He tucked the blanket more securely around her shoulders. Dark circles had formed under her eyes. Thin blue veins stood out against her closed eyelids. She hadn't had enough sleep—she had cried too much.

Last night had been rough. From almost zero knowledge about her father to nearly absolute certainty within a single day; it was enough to make his head spin. No wonder she was highly emotional.

He and his siblings had been fortunate in the family he was born into. As Krista said, he'd been secure in the knowledge of who he was, where he came from. Sean and Giulia had provided that security for their children. No matter how far away he and his brothers traveled, they'd always come back home.

Blake wanted that with Krista. A home of their own. Be it here or in the Philippines, it didn't matter, as long as they were together.

Selfishly, he wanted Uncle Jack to wake up. So Krista could meet her father. So her father could acknowledge her. So Blake could finally propose.

Maybe I should call Ronan to get an update.

Just as Blake reached for his phone, it rang.

"Baby, wake up." He shook her shoulder with one hand as he thumbed the answer key on the phone with the other. "It's Ronan."

Krista bolted upright, instantly alert.

"Blake, *Ate* Krista, Dad's awake," the younger O'Connor son announced. His excited voice rang clearly through the airwaves. Blake had put him on speaker.

"Thank God," Krista whispered reverently.

"He's undergoing tests right now, but he should be able to accept visitors in a few hours, say around four or five. I took personal time off. *Kuya* Patrick and I will help at the pub tonight. We spoke with Mom—she's expecting you."

"We'll be there," Blake replied before pressing the off button. Krista was beaming beside him, her joy unmistakable.

"He's awake. I can see him."

"Yes, sweetheart. You can finally see him."

***

The massive bronze door that marked the entrance to the south transept of St. Patrick's Cathedral, the largest Gothic church in New York City, opened to admit more tourists. Before it closed again, a circle of light fell over Krista's bowed head through the stained-glass Founder's Window, giving her a halo. She knelt in front of the Altar of Our Lady of Guadalupe, a rosary in her hand, oblivious to the heavenly blessing she'd received.

Blake sat on a pew several feet behind, smiling. Krista had managed to bring him to a church again. They'd gone in Boracay, in Makati, and now here in New York. A feat only his mother was able to accomplish for many years.

Krista made the sign of the cross and kissed the crucifix at the end of the rosary, signaling the end of her prayers.

Blake rose to his feet, stepped to the side, and genuflected. When he stood upright again, Krista was beside him, staring.

"Do I have something on my face?" He rubbed his jaw where stubble had started to grow.

"No. I love it when you come to church with me. I feel a million times blessed."

"Only a million?" he teased. "I feel a gazillion." He tapped her nose. "Are you ready to meet him?"

"Yes," she said. "I'm glad we came here instead of waiting at the hospital." Krista beamed at him. "I needed to give thanks for the miracles of healing and discovery. God is good." After another look around, she turned and led the way to the door.

They exited onto 51st Street. From there, the taxi they hailed had a straight route to Tenth Avenue. Even with the afternoon traffic, they arrived at the hospital in less than ten minutes.

"Do you know his room?" Krista asked as they entered the main lobby.

"Yes. He's in the Deluxe Accommodations wing, but *Tita* Belen wants to talk to you first. She's waiting for us in the cafeteria."

Tita Belen sat at a table in a corner of the room. Blake kissed the cheek she proffered. "Please sit beside me, Krista. I want to thank you."

"You're welcome, but what did I do that you're grateful for?" Krista asked, sitting beside Belen as directed. Blake chose the seat to his girlfriend's left.

"I was there when they transfused John after his second surgery. The bag had a different label on it than the previous ones. Beside the computerized donor code somebody wrote KL by hand. His condition rapidly improved after that. You saved his life." *Tita* Belen clasped Krista's hands in hers. "Before that, I was told they were running low on B negative, even after they'd already asked the Red Cross for more supply. My boys confirmed that you donated for Jack. *Salamat, Anak.*"

The words "thank you, my child" brought tears to Krista's eyes. Blake had to blink away the moisture in his.

"You're welcome *po* ... uhm, Mrs. O'Connor."

"Please, call me *Tita* Belen."

"*Tita* Belen," Krista dutifully repeated.

"I also asked Dr. Vasquez to run a paternity test using your blood. She was telling me John was not excluded as your father at the exact moment he woke up. He knows he has a daughter. He wants to meet you."

Tears filled Krista's eyes. "I want to meet him too. When?"

"We can go now." *Tita* Belen stood. "They just moved him to his own room. I wanted to talk to you before you meet. I'd like to apologize for my rudeness yesterday. Seeing you brought back bad memories and made me doubt John all over again, like I did before we got married."

"No apologies necessary. I understand. *Tita* Belen, may Blake go with us? I want him there with me when I meet my father for the first time."

"Of course he may," *Tita* Belen said graciously. She leaned closer to Krista and stage-whispered, "Don't tell the others, but Blake is my favorite of the Ryan kids. We have the same birthday." The wink she gave Krista made all of them laugh.

Blake smiled broadly. He'd wanted this lighthearted teasing and the instant rapport for *Tita* Belen and Krista's first meeting. The opposite had happened; it made him happy to see it now.

CHAPTER THIRTEEN
Manhattan

Krista gripped Blake's hand so tight, she was afraid she'd break his bones. The nearer they got to the room where she'd meet her father, the faster her heartbeat galloped against her ribcage. She hadn't thought she would be this nervous.

"Relax, sweetheart. Uncle Jack's a great guy. He's going to love you."

"Promise?"

"Promise, pinky swear, cross my heart," he teased.

Tita Belen opened the door and poked her head in before turning back to Krista and Blake. "He's up." She opened the door wide. "Come in."

"Go on, I'm behind you." Blake pressed his lips to her head and gave her a small push forward.

John was sitting up in bed. Even with his skin pale, his eyes cloudy with pain, and numerous IVs all over his arms, he still attempted to smile. "Come, child. I was told you saved my life. Blake, it's great to see you, son."

Krista positioned herself beside the bed and laid her hand on top of his right arm, in between two IV lines. "I'm glad I was able to help." Though she smiled at him, she couldn't tear her eyes away from his scar.

It was faint now, not as angry as it was in that photo, but still there.

"Krista; a lovely name. Tell me about yourself, your family." He spoke slowly, pausing after every other word.

"I was born in Pampanga, in a small town called Santa Rita. My mother and her husband, my adoptive father, moved there from Angeles City when she was pregnant with me. I have two siblings, a sister and a brother." Krista had tried to prepare for this meeting, but she found herself babbling now that the moment had finally arrived.

"Forgive me if my memory fails me: what did your mother say about how we met?" A look passed between husband and wife after he asked the question. Apologetic on his side, understanding on hers.

"She said you rescued her from three men outside the restaurant where she worked. They were drunk and ..." Krista couldn't continue. The horror of what could have happened to her mother if John hadn't come along was too unthinkable.

"Oh, John," *Tita* Belen cried out. "She must have been terrified. What's your mother's name, *Anak*?

"Marissa *po*. She's about your height. *Mestiza*. She always kept her hair long, past her waist." Krista hoped that description would jog John's memory.

John visibly started, his right hand lifting to the scar above his right eye.

"I insisted on escorting her home. She patched me up." He looked at Krista, then his wife. "She couldn't stop shaking. Still replaying in her mind what almost happened. I wanted to show her the act didn't have to be brutal." John's mouth turned down. "We slept. My internal alarm clock woke me up. There was a curfew at the base at the time. Two hundred hours. I didn't have time to write a note. I was facing being declared AWOL."

Krista's heart rejoiced, even as she strove hard not to show it. Her mother had told her the same story, almost word for word. "She tried to find you, but she didn't have access to the base. She waited until she couldn't. When she started to show, she married her suitor—my *tatay*—and they moved to a different town."

John shut his eyes, as if pained by the memory. "I was deployed for six months. When I returned, she no longer worked at the restaurant. Nobody knew where she went." Tears seeped from his closed lids. "No one told me about a child." When he opened his eyes, they were full of regret. "I never knew about you, Krista. Forgive me, my daughter."

Krista nearly started bawling. She felt an overwhelming sense of joy. There it was. His acknowledgment of her. The one thing she'd prayed for after she found out he was going to live.

She squeezed his arm, careful not to jostle him too much. "There is nothing to forgive ... Father. You were both victims of circumstance. What's important is now, and how we move on from here."

"So young, so wise. Must have gotten it from your mother. The only thing I could give you was my good looks," he joked, flashing the charm that must have been potent when he was younger.

He moved his arm and turned his hand over, asking her silently to hold it. She complied. "Krista, I know I don't deserve it, and I hope I can make up for thirty years of absence in the near future, but it would please me if you called me Dad."

"Dad," she repeated, testing the word out. "Dad," she said louder, with more conviction. It felt good to say it out loud.

"Thank you." Her dad relaxed back on his pillows. He was getting tired. They should go.

"Where is your mother now?" *Tita* Belen asked. Her gaze held mild curiosity, no jealousy reflected there.

"*Nanay* and *Tatay* now live in Lucena City in Quezon. They own and operate a roadside café there."

"Krista, your mother Marissa, is she also a cook?" *Tita* Belen asked.

"*Opo, Tita.*" She looked at her dad. "She said she was one when you met in Angeles City."

"John, you have a type," his wife teased.

"I did, *mahal*." His left hand closed over his wife's. The look they exchanged was tender.

I did, love. In the past. No longer.

Krista looked back at Blake, who stood behind her as he'd promised. Her eyes shining with hope, she held tight to his hand on her shoulder.

There it was. She knew it. The Irish-American and Filipina couple whose relationship they could emulate. *That's us in thirty years.*

***

Krista paced in front of Jack O'Connor's pictures at the pub. Even though there were enough hands, she and Blake had decided to help with the dinner service. Their conversation had exhausted Jack, so they'd left with promises to return the next day for more catching up.

She also wanted to call her mother, to tell her she'd found her biological father and show her his photo. It was already Sunday in the Philippines. The café would be closed, and her parents would be home after attending mass. They'd relax before Marissa started preparations for *noche buena*, the midnight meal that was a Filipino Christmas Eve tradition.

Krista had texted her sister as soon as she and Blake arrived at Ryan O'Connor's. She'd asked Farrah to let her know when she could do a video call with them. That was five minutes ago; no response yet.

Blake opened the door. "Nothing yet?"

"No. It's Christmas Eve, on a Sunday. Maybe the mass went long."

He chuckled. "Ah, yes. The two-hour long Filipino masses. I've been to a couple of those."

She slapped his arm without much force. He'd spoken true. In her excitement, she'd forgotten about the Filipino Catholic traditions.

There would have been a dramatization of the birth of Christ, starting with a couple playing Mary and Joseph entering Bethlehem, seeking a place to stay the night. The play would end at the stable where Jesus was born. Traditionally, the play continued during the midnight mass, with a full choir proclaiming *Gloria in Excelsis Deo.*

Krista watched Blake as he sat down behind the desk. He looked good there, the consummate businessman. "What are you going to tell them?" He leaned back in the chair and folded his arms behind his head.

Tired of pacing, she sat. "That I've found John. They'd know what it means, particularly my mom." She hadn't prepared a speech; she just planned to state the facts.

"If you say 'found,' that means you've been looking for him. Have you?"

Frowning at Blake, she replied, "Not actively, no. I've often wondered, but I didn't know where to begin. I didn't know I wanted to find him until I got here, and the pieces began to fit." Krista started to feel irritated with her boyfriend. "Why are you asking this now? You know the answer."

Blake stood and walked around the desk. He sat on his haunches and held her hands. "Baby, I like and respect Uncle Jack. I'm glad he's your biological father."

She could hear a "but" coming on.

"I also like and respect *Tito* Arsenio. He's been your father for thirty years, Uncle Jack for only a couple of hours. Just be careful how you phrase your news, is what I'm trying to say." Blake turned her hands over and dropped a kiss on the center of each palm. He laid his head on her lap.

Oh. Krista absently combed her fingers through Blake's hair, mulling his words. He was right. She had planned to announce it exactly the way she told Blake. She'd found her father.

Her father had never been lost. Her *tatay* had always been there for her and her mother. She might have John O'Connor's genes, but she'd had Arsenio Lopez's love even longer than she'd been alive.

Krista leaned down to give Blake a brief kiss. "I'm the luckiest girl in the world. Some people don't even have one, but I have two fathers. I've loved the first all my life, and now I'm looking forward to getting to know the second. Thanks for reminding me."

She reached for the phone when it beeped. "Do you want to stay with me while I talk to them?"

Blake was already on his feet. "Sure. I'll practice my Tagalog. *Maligayang Pasko, po. Tito* Arsen *at Tita* Marissa. *Kumusta*, Farrah? *Kumusta*, Alex?" He singsonged the Filipino greetings for Merry Christmas and hello.

"You're crazy."

"Crazy for youuuuu," he crooned to the tune of Madonna's eighties hit, making her giggle. She needed five more minutes before she could video chat with her family.

"*Nanay, Tatay*, Merry Christmas *po*," Krista greeted her parents when their images appeared. She used Blake's tablet instead of her phone to call her family, to see them better on the wide screen. Blake waved from behind her and said his practiced Tagalog words.

"*Maligayang Pasko, Anak.* You're quite early, *ha*," her mother remarked.

"*Opo*, I wanted to greet you before the networks get too busy with overseas calls. I know you need to get ready soon for the carolers and the neighborhood kids asking for their *pamasko*." Once their financial circumstances had improved, since Alex graduated from college, her parents had started the tradition of giving away wrapped presents to children under twelve.

"*May balita ka ba, Anak?*" her *tatay* said teasingly, asking her in Filipino if she had any important news to share.

Krista was intrigued when Blake made slashing motions with his finger across his throat, then gestured forward. On the other side, her adoptive father indicated his understanding by raising both thumbs in the air.

Assuming the two were done with their male bonding, Krista spoke again. "Actually, I do have news. I met someone today. I wanted to share this with you right away because this is important to me. *He* is important to me." Without giving her parents a chance to speak or herself time to chicken out, she switched the camera to the rear-view, to her biological father's pilot photo.

"*Nanay*, I met John."

Krista watched as her mother's face paled in shock.

"*O, Dios ko*. That *is* John." She was so surprised, she took the Lord's name in vain. Marissa gaped at the camera as Krista panned to the other pictures, pausing lengthily at the one with the fresh scar. She visibly jumped when *Tatay* placed his arm around her shoulders. She tore her gaze away from the photos and turned to her husband. Cupping his face with both hands, she whispered, "Arsen." A tender smile crossed *Tatay*'s face. He brushed his lips against her forehead and whispered her name just as softly, "Marissa."

A lump formed in Krista's throat at the sight of her parents' affection. She switched the camera back.

Clearing her throat, her *nanay* faced her again. "How did you meet him? Where was he?"

She and Blake had discussed not mentioning the stabbing and attempted theft, so Krista replied, "Here, at the pub co-owned by Blake's parents. John and his wife are the other owners. His full name is John Jackson O'Connor."

"What a small world *talaga, ano*?" A note of wonder entered her mother's tone. "I'm happy for you, *Anak*." Marisa Lopez held hands with her husband. "I'm glad you met your father on Christmas. That's a wonderful blessing."

Krista's eyes gleamed when they met Blake's. "Truly, *Nanay*. A wonderful blessing, indeed." Her mother's reaction pleased her. It didn't surprise her at all. She knew her love for Arsenio Lopez was deep-abiding. John was a short chapter, Krista's *tatay* the whole book. "Enjoy your Christmas, *'Nay, 'Tay. Mahal ko po kayo*." Krista signed off by telling them she loved them.

CHAPTER FOURTEEN

Lady Liberty

The crowned female figure, draped in a green robe with a book tucked in her left arm and a torch raised in her right hand, had welcomed millions of immigrants to the United States of America for over one hundred and thirty years. The Statue of Liberty greeted Krista now as she and Blake and a couple of hundred revelers awaited the fireworks that would signal the arrival of the new year from aboard a boat idling in the New York Harbor.

Her eyes shone as she beheld one of the symbols that represented New York City—the entire USA—to the world. It was among the must-visit places on her list, along with the Empire State Building, Times Square, and St. Patrick's Cathedral. They'd gone to the others in the past week—the 9-11 Memorial, the Rockefeller Center, a matinee performance of Hamilton on Broadway, and they'd even taken a day trip to the Hamptons—but they'd saved Lady Liberty for last. She and Blake were set to return to the Philippines in three days.

Krista breathed deeply, glad the cold dulled her sense of smell when she sniffed the brine of the Atlantic Ocean mixed with alcohol and the perfumes of the partygoers. Shuddering at the thought of doing this in the summer, she tugged her hood forward to cover her face.

The forecast had said fifteen degrees Fahrenheit with not much wind, one of the reasons they chose this custom cruise instead of the horse-drawn carriage in Central Park.

Krista had come to New York to meet the Ryans. All she'd wanted when she arrived was for Blake's family to like her. On her first day, they'd done more than that: they'd convinced her that they wanted her to *be* a Ryan.

Then, after the unthinkable had happened, the biggest coincidence of all: she met her biological father the next day. She and Jack O'Connor had attempted to forge a bond in a few days that should have been made over thirty years.

Only when her dad was discharged from the hospital on Boxing Day did Blake and *Tita* Belen celebrate their joint birthday. They'd closed the pub at nine and had fun taking turns in front of the mic.

Krista grinned, remembering Dad's attempts to sing. She'd certainly gotten *that* talent from her mother. Jack O'Connor's voice could send dogs howling. Everyone enjoyed the party so much, they'd planned another for January 2nd, a farewell dinner for Krista and Blake, Aidan, and Craig.

Jack O'Connor was given strict instructions not to overdo the exertion, so Blake still managed the books and Krista assisted in the kitchen so that *Tita* Belen could go home early. Starting on New Year's Day, the older Ryans and O'Connors planned to turn over the closing hours to a manager. The four owners wanted to leave before midnight every night from now on.

Krista and Blake had also checked out of The Plaza upon the insistence of his parents. Giulia and Sean were aghast at the idea of them spending thousands of dollars on a place they barely stayed in. Blake's bedroom at his parents' house was adequate for sleeping, but hardly conducive to romantic moments.

She started when a champagne flute appeared in front of her face.

"Tell me again whose crazy idea it was to freeze our butts off on New Year's Eve?" Blake nudged her earmuff aside with his lips to mutter in her ear. "What's his name? I'll kick his ass."

Krista accepted the glass and turned around to face him. "Blake Ryan, Boracay has spoiled you. You're now a cold-weather wuss." She poked his cleft chin with her gloved finger.

"I am. I admit it. I'd rather swim in that clear balmy water, sunbathe on the powdery white sand, sip mango shakes, and make love with you in the hammock than shiver in this damnable cold."

Krista's breath caught at the evocative images he conjured with his words. She took a sip of the champagne to cool her suddenly heated body.

Before she went to Boracay for her thirtieth birthday, she didn't like the beach, and she hated getting dark. A funny attitude for someone born in an archipelago. It took a foreigner—an American, for her to appreciate the beauty her birth country had to offer.

She cleared her throat. "We'll be home soon. Maybe we'll go to Perlas during the weekend of Valentine's Day, too."

"Then Holy Week in March, Labor Day in May, Philippine Independence Day in June. And the Fourth of July—"

"Not the Fourth of July," Krista interrupted. "I promised Dad we'll come back here for his birthday." A note of petulance had crept into her voice.

Blake peered at her face, sensing her mood change. He cursed when somebody bumped into him. The other passengers had come out onto the deck, seeking prime positions for viewing the fireworks.

"Let's go." He took her elbow and steered her towards the cabin.

Krista approved. They were on the upper deck and could still see the fireworks through the roof and port holes without the noise of the explosions to deafen them. People milled around, but there were fewer bodies here than outside. They could talk.

Blake led her to the bow side of the room where a free table conveniently awaited them. Cushioned seats lined the wall on one side. A round table for two held two glasses and a wine chiller containing a bottle of champagne. Similar arrangements were scattered throughout the room.

She removed her winter gear and dropped it on the seat. Blake did the same before sitting down and pulling her onto his lap.

"Honey," Krista admonished him.

"I don't care. They don't either. I want to hold you. I haven't done a lot of that during this vacation." He punctuated his words by nuzzling her neck and hugging her tight. After another squeeze, he loosened his hold. "Okay, tell me."

"Tell you what?"

"Why you don't want to go back to Boracay."

"I do want to go to Boracay, just not every month."

"Why not?" He seemed genuinely confused.

Krista held his face and looked into his eyes. "Because if we do, it'll lose its special meaning. It'll just be another place. Do you know what I mean?"

Blake brushed a lock of hair from her face. "I do." His finger traced her features as if he was learning them for the first time. "Is Boracay special to you?"

"Yes," she breathed. His finger traced her lips.

"Why?"

"Because that's where we fell in love," she said huskily.

He brought his hand down from her face. She moaned at the loss of contact.

When he spoke again his voice was gravelly, as if he had a lump in his throat. "So, Boracay is somewhere we should be celebrating momentous events in our life. Is that what you mean?"

Krista nodded. His intensity was palpable. He was almost vibrating beneath her. Outside, uniformed servers refilled champagne glasses and distributed noisemakers. Through the bottom of her high-heeled boots, she felt the sway of the boat.

"A momentous event like our wedding." Blake held up a ring between his fingers. The heart-shaped diamond in the center was cradled by two hands, one on each side. Three small diamonds formed a crown over the heart.

She teared up and smiled at the same time.

"This was my mother's Claddagh ring, given to her by my father. I asked her for it. Nothing in the stores could match its meaning for me. Ma told us boys that it will go to the first of us to fall in love. She said to only give it to the woman who holds my heart in her hands. That's you. Maria Krista Lopez, will you marry me?" He put the ring on her finger.

"Yes, Blake Henry Ryan. I will treasure it and care for it, but not as much as I will treasure and care for your love. For our love. I love you, and I'll marry you."

Both reached for the other at the same time, lips meeting in a kiss filled with promises.

Three.

Two.

One.

Everywhere around them, people kissed and sang *Auld Lang Syne*, fireworks exploded, and the new year began. For Krista and Blake, it was more than a new year; it was the beginning of a new life. Together.

EPILOGUE

Blake grinned as the women in his family flocked around Krista to admire her engagement ring. They'd come straight to the pub for their farewell party after an overnight trip to Niagara Falls. Unlike his and *Tita* Belen's birthday celebration, the parents decided to keep Ryan O'Connor's regular hours; they'd blocked off a section for the family, but welcomed customers in. At ten in the evening on the second day of the new year, the place was full.

He stood in the corner, waiting for Krista to signal him if the ladies started talking about the wedding. Judging by the gleam in his mother's eyes, she was determined to take part in the planning. His fiancée could hold her own, but they'd agreed to answer questions together.

Aidan sidled up beside him, his eyes also on the table of laughing women—their mom, *Tita* Belen, Darcy, and Krista. "Thanks for getting me off the hook."

"I didn't do it for you." Blake nearly laughed at his brother. Aidan was delusional if he really thought he was saved from getting questioned about settling down. At best, Blake had only given him a reprieve. Their Ma would be dropping hints again as soon as he and Krista set their plans.

"Are you talking about the wedding tonight?"

Blake narrowed his eyes at his brother's overly casual tone. Aidan had been engrossed with this topic for days now. "We'll start some of it now, but we won't finalize anything until Krista has met with her family and friends in Manila." Friends. Her best friend in particular. *Oh ho!* "She'll want to ask them what role they want to play in the wedding. Maybe she'll ask her sister, Farrah, to be the maid of honor."

Aidan shrugged. "That's her choice to make."

Blake tried another tack. "I wonder who Maddie will bring to the wedding. I've met her new boss. French, smooth and cultured. Same age as you."

Aidan growled out a response that sounded like, "Surrender monkeys."

Blake grinned. "She's half-French. I'd be careful what you call them around her."

"Who said anything about seeing Madeleine?"

"Singapore is a small place. I'm sure you'll bump into her." Blake didn't wait for Aidan to respond. He strode to the table and sat beside his fiancée. She had winked: their prearranged signal.

The dads came out of the office and took their customary seats at the opposite ends of the long table. Uncle Jack had been out of a wheelchair since New Year's Eve. Though still pale, he'd already lost the haggard look from his hospital stay.

"Where is everyone?" Blake asked the group.

Darcy, the Little Ms. I-Know-Where-The-O'Connor-Brothers-Are-At-All-Times, had the answer. "Patrick is in Hawaii for the Tournament of Champions. Ronan said he'll drop by if he's in this area."

"Craig told me he'll come out here after he has expedited the last order of the night." This time it was *Tita* Belen who replied. "We can start without them."

Taking it as a signal, Da began the prayer.

The moment amen was uttered, Giulia launched her questions. "Have you decided yet where and when you're getting married?"

Blake held Krista's hand on top of the table. They'd already discussed this during their trip upstate. "We want to have a church wedding in Boracay, and if you'll all agree …" he paused, looking at each of the elders separately, "we'd like to have our annual reunion celebration there at the same time."

"A Christmas wedding! How wonderful." Ma clasped her hands in front of her chest. "Sean?" she beseeched Da.

"All right. These old bones could use some thawing," Da said, winking at Krista. She grinned back at him. Blake brought their entwined hands to his lips, pleased that his fiancée had quickly become close with his family.

His voice husky, Uncle Jack replied, "It's the first special event of my daughter's life I will have the opportunity to witness. We wouldn't miss it for the world."

Krista stood to move to her dad's side. She kissed his cheek and *Tita* Belen's. "Thank you. It will mean so much to me for you to be there." They responded by hugging her tight.

Craig approached the table with a tray of champagne-filled flutes. "Compliments of the owners."

Tita Belen rose to her feet. Raising her glass, she said, "To Krista and Blake, the first wedding in the Ryan and O'Connor families ..."

Ma jumped up and looking pointedly at her oldest son, she quipped, "... may it only be the beginning."

"Hear, hear," Blake cheered, earning him a glare from Aidan and a giggle from Krista.

Everyone stood and clinked glasses. "To Krista and Blake. *Sláinte.*"

AUTHOR'S NOTE

When I first came to the US in 1994 as an exchange visitor with the Girl Scouts/YMCA, my first stop was New York. I've been back three times since then and whenever I visit this remarkably vibrant place, I always have a wonderful time. They say you never forget your first, that's why The City That Never Sleeps holds a special place in my heart.

I hope you enjoyed the continuation of Krista and Blake's story in NEW YORK ENGAGEMENT. There's more to come for my favorite couple (so far), but what? They'll let me know and I'll be sure to share their story with you.

In case you haven't read BORACAY VOWS yet, you'll be able to purchase it from your favorite etailer. https://books2read.com/Boracay-Vows

Maddie and Aidan's love story is told in two parts: the prequel novelette GLOBAL CITY TRYST and the full-length novel SINGAPORE FLING. Both are available now. https://books2read.com/GlobalCityTryst and https://books2read.com/SingaporeFling

For bonus content, check out my website www.maidamalby.com. You'll find photos of all the places and food I mentioned in the series, as well as sneak peeks of my work-in-progress. Subscribe to my newsletter (maidamalby.com/newsletter) for book promotions, signing events, cover reveals, and ARC opportunities. If you have any questions or comments, you can contact me at maida@maidamalby.com. You can also find me on Facebook (Maida Malby), Twitter (@MaidaMalby), and Instagram (@maidamalbyauthor). And if you liked my book, please leave a review. I'd really appreciate it and it'll help new readers find it. Thank you.